ALSO BY PETER TAYLOR

A Summons to Memphis

Peter Taylor

A SUMMONS
TO MEMPHIS

ALFRED A. KNOPF

New York 1986

F
TAY

Library of Congress Cataloging-in-Publication Data
Taylor, Peter Hillsman, [date]
A summons to Memphis.
I. Title.
PS3539.A9633S8   1986   813'.54   86-45417
ISBN 0-394-41062-9

Manufactured in the United States of America
First Edition

For Eleanor, Katie and Ross

With love

A SUMMONS TO MEMPHIS

1

THE COURTSHIP and remarriage of an old widower is always made more difficult when middle-aged children are involved—especially when there are unmarried daughters. This seemed particularly true in the landlocked, backwater city of Memphis some forty-odd years ago. At least it is a certainty that remarriage was more difficult for old widowers in Memphis than it was over in Nashville, say, or in Knoxville—or even in Chattanooga, for that matter. One needs to know those other cities only slightly to be absolutely sure of this. Yet one cannot say with equal certainty just why the difficulty was so peculiar to Memphis, unless it is that Memphis, unlike the other Tennessee cities, remains to this day a "land-oriented" place. Nearly everybody there who is anybody is apt still to own some land. He owns it in Arkansas or in West Tennessee or in the Mississippi Delta. And it may be that whenever or wherever land gets involved, any family matter is bound to become more complex, less reasonable, more desperate.

At any rate, during the time when I was in my teens and had recently been removed from Nashville to Memphis, one was always hearing of some old widower or other whose watchful, middle-aged children had set out to save him from an ill-considered second marriage. The would-be bride-to-be in those cases was frequently vilified by the family to all who would listen. If matters got sufficiently out of hand, the question of the old widower's sanity was often raised. The middle-aged children themselves were either pitied or were held up to ridicule—for the simple reason that they now of course would not likely come into an inheritance. To my family, so recently arrived in Memphis from Nashville, this seemed a vulgar and utterly ridiculous human situation. We were not accustomed to people's airing their personal problems so publicly. My father had not as a matter of fact wished to move us to Memphis at all. He would not have done so had he not been deceived and nearly ruined financially by his closest friend and principal legal client back in Nashville, one Mr. Lewis Shackleford. But the fact was, Father did not wish to continue living in the same city with a man so faithless and dishonest as Lewis Shackleford. Father was, himself, a lawyer of the highest standing and knew that his reputation would precede him to Memphis. And so he quietly removed his wife and his four children to the banks of the Mississippi, where we his family would be expected to cope with the peculiar institutions of the place—the institutions, that is to say, which one associates with the cotton and river culture of the Deep South. This removal and readjustment required a tremendous effort for us all and was a strain one way or another on everybody. And yet on the whole the move was made quietly and without fanfare, in the best Upper South manner. There was nothing Deep South about our family—an important distinction in our minds. Father made no public denunciation of the

man who had betrayed him and who had made the move necessary. Instead, that man's name simply became a name that
was not allowed to be spoken aloud in our new Memphis
household.

Almost immediately upon arrival in Memphis, this Nashville family of ours heard the news of a rich old widower in
our very neighborhood who had taken a notion to remarry
and who was being denounced and persecuted by his own
middle-aged children. The image of that old man was for me
one that I would carry sempiternally in my head even until
the present time, as some kind of symbol, I suppose, of Memphis itself—a rich old Memphis father, that is, the provisions
of his will already well known, deciding suddenly to take
unto himself a second wife and thus changing the prospects
of everybody concerned, an utterly selfish act on the old
man's part with no care for past family tradition and no
thought of how his descendants would regard him. To complete this picture in my head of this symbolic Memphis situation there were, of course, the inevitable middle-aged children
coming forward in force—and possibly some of the grown-up
grandchildren—coming forward, that is, to assert that they
would not countenance such a step on the part of their rich
and selfish old widower-father, who cared more for his own
gratification and comfort than for the name and honor of the
family. Alas, it was a picture we would see depicted all too
frequently during the early years of our life there on the
banks of the Mississippi River.

WHEN MY OLD mother died two years ago it did not
at first occur to me that we could have any such difficulty
amongst ourselves. We were not after all a genuine Memphis
family. We had lived in Memphis only thirty years. There

were, moreover, no grandchildren—in whose names all claims against the father and all justifications of the middle-aged children's behavior were usually made. And my father had long since divested himself of his own landholdings in upper West Tennessee. Further, I had myself been living off here in Manhattan for more than two decades. The whole matter seemed very remote to me. My only brother was long since dead in the Second War. And my two unmarried, elder sisters were well established in an immensely successful business venture. They seemed much too proud and too fond of Father to express criticism openly of any course the old gentleman might follow.

The fact was, within weeks after Mother's death and funeral, my sisters began playfully teasing Father about the various old ladies of his acquaintance, those who were inviting him to dine rather regularly. This seemed to me a very healthy sign. My closest friend there in Memphis, Alex Mercer, wrote me at the time how much he admired the way Betsy and Josephine were conducting themselves. There was no evidence, Alex assured me, of their taking a protective or defensive role of any kind. And then within a matter of two or three months Alex wrote me to express new admiration for my sisters. Father's social life had by then taken a different turn. The dear old man had begun to appear at nightclubs and bars, not with the old ladies, of course, but with "young-ish women" of a very different sort from those ladies who had him to dine. My friend Alex found this shocking and some-what disturbing to himself in a personal way since he had always been one of Father's greatest admirers. But as for my middle-aged sisters, they seemed to delight in this new turn also. And this seemed to me most gratifying. They even wrote me about all of this and said they hoped I might be as broad-minded as they were. It seemed to me a wonderful eventuality to contemplate. Who could ask for more? It seemed highly civilized. But when, after two more months had passed, Father's interest took a still different turn and he began showing attentions to a respectable but undistinguished and schoolteacherish woman he had met, my sisters knew not where, a woman named Mrs. Clara Stockwell, it was then an altogether different story with Betsy and Josephine. It was then that I, off in Manhattan, received my two separate telephone calls from my sisters, both of them urging me to fly to Memphis at once in order to help prevent our old father from making a fatal mistake. I must say, my sisters' behavior now sounded like the same old Memphis phenomenon. I could scarcely believe it was happening to *us*, and happening in this day and age besides, and happening in a city like modern-day Memphis, which is no longer a little city of two hundred thousand souls but a sprawling metropolis nearer to nine hundred thousand.

When I received my two sisters' long-distance calls—within twenty minutes of each other—it was a dark, late Sunday afternoon in March, and I was alone in my Manhattan apartment. I did not at once commit myself to coming to Memphis next day and from the very first I was not sure I wished to participate at all in their campaign against Father. I was astonished of course by their sudden about-face, but it seemed understandable in some degree. The old ladies and the youngish women had not of course been the threat to Father's single state that a sensible woman like Mrs. Clara Stockwell was. But still, any alleged justification aside, I wished to know what precisely my sisters' procedure in their interference would be. It seemed to me that they had not the resources at hand that similar middle-aged children used once to have. That is, filial authority was not what it once had been in dealing with the very old. And yet in the course of their telephone calls that Sunday twilight I thought I had detected an old-fashioned fury in my sisters' voices which made me fearful for my father's well-being.

AS I HAVE SAID, I was alone in my apartment when the two calls came. And my solitary condition at the time is worth mentioning. It had more than a little to do with the decision I would ultimately make about flying down to Memphis. My life in New York, you will understand, is very different indeed from that of my family in Memphis. I had left home before I was thirty, a young man not long back from World War II. I had been living for several years now in my present apartment with a woman friend named Holly Kaplan. (Holly was fifteen years younger than I, and I was forty-nine at the time I speak of.) But on the previous Sunday, Holly had moved out. She had moved out after those dozen years of our living here together. I mention this to help explain why I was in the frame of mind I was and why I would respond as I did to the news of what seemed about to happen to my father. Holly Kaplan, as a matter of fact, would return here to live after only a few weeks' separation, and she and I have lived here in relative contentment since, she continuing to work at her magazine office and I engrossed as ever in my concerns as rare-book collector and as an editor at the publishing house with which I have been associated for twenty years. Our orderly life together here—Holly's and mine—is still as different as it could conceivably be from the life of my family in Memphis or, for that matter, from the life of Holly's Jewish family in Cleveland.

Anyway, for the several months past, Holly and I had been nagging at each other and contradicting each other rather endlessly—apparently over almost nothing. I think perhaps we were simply another case of the middle-aged doldrums, which must be the same whether it involves sensible people like us, living unwed together in New York, or less fortunate people caught in a foolish marriage back in Memphis or Cleveland. When my sisters' telephone calls came through that Sunday, it was after a week of bitter-cold weather, with snow falling half of every day. Ugly gray banks of it, now frozen solid, impeded most movement on the sidewalks below. I had no desire to be out in it. Betsy's call came on the very stroke of five during the dreary Sunday twilight. Jo's call would come barely twenty minutes after Betsy's was concluded.

For two days I had not been out of the apartment. When I was not going over manuscripts and proof sheets I suppose I was wondering what it was that was wrong between Holly and me. Neither of us knew why things had gone so sour, why the satisfaction had gone out of our formerly serene existence together. For weeks and months we had kept going over the particulars of our systematic, well-ordered life, expecting to find the trouble in some element of our life that was perhaps just too obvious for us to see.

Each accused the other of having an interest in someone else. There *was*, as a matter of fact, a new girl in my publishing office whom I found very attractive. I tried to examine my motives to determine if subconsciously I was allowing that to affect my behavior with Holly. But there was nothing to it. Possibly Holly examined her own motives, too, and no doubt found herself innocent. Anyhow, there had seemed nothing for it but that we should have a trial separation. Within only two or three days after Holly had gone I knew there was nothing to be gained by our living apart. I thought of how it would be to spend the rest of my life alone, as I had done when I first came to New York. I saw myself traipsing down that little corridor every morning from bedroom to kitchen and back to my study and settling in to my work without a word from anybody. (I never went to my publishing office till afternoon.) It was a gloomy prospect. Already I could not bear the sight of the new girl in my office. And of course the weekend was the worst time. It was under those circumstances that I received the calls from Memphis.

When the telephone rang and I presently heard Betsy's voice on the other end, I was aware that I had never before been so glad to hear the voice of either of my sisters. But I was at once puzzled and uneasy too, because Betsy and Josephine Carver are women of a generation for whom a long-distance telephone call, outside of business, can mean but one thing. It means, to say the least, a family crisis. My sisters are of a generation that came of age during the vicissitudes of the Great Depression. For our family those vicissitudes were great indeed. It meant—because of Mr. Lewis Shackleford, my father's deceiver and betrayer—moving from a handsome estate on the Franklin Pike south of Nashville to a rather plain city house in midtown Memphis. No matter how affluent my sisters and my father had since become, neither Betsy nor Jo would ever forget to be saving about things like leaving on lights in an empty room, like running the furnace while away from home, like making needless long-distance telephone calls. In their hearts and minds they still lived in the days of the old Depression of the thirties. Perhaps this contributed to the enormous success they were to have in the insurance and real estate agency they would eventually form together. But I can't speak with authority about that since I am not, myself, a businessman. I was of the same generation as my sisters, of course, but of a totally different temperament, let us say, and perhaps enough younger not to have felt the full force of the lessons the Depression taught them. Immediately upon hearing my sister Betsy's voice I asked into the phone: "Is anything wrong, Betsy?" There was a silence during which I could almost see her face, particularly her mouth as she bit first her upper and then her lower lip, trying to decide whether it would be better to break her news gradually or abruptly. She decided on the former, I suppose.

"Yes, Phillip," she declared, lifting her voice a whole octave. "It's about Father."

There was another silence. And I think I felt a certain glee. During all that long, lonely week since Holly's departure I had felt so low that it seemed momentarily I was really glad there was somebody in Memphis who had something wrong too. Then I told myself it wasn't only that. Rather, I was simply happy to have a distraction of any kind whatsoever from my morbid thoughts about my future of living alone. I felt I could never persuade another young woman like Holly Kaplan to move in and share quarters with me. My receding hairline, my stooped shoulders, my slovenly way of dressing all precluded that. And so as I spoke into the telephone I quickly changed my tone. I was prepared to be distracted and amused. "What is it, Betsy?" I asked. "What in the world is wrong?"

Now there was another silence on Betsy's part. She was debating further how best to tell me. This hesitation was cause for concern, because neither of my sisters is given to hesitation over what to say or how to say it. Finally she could resist no longer plunging right into the matter: "It's Father, Phillip. Your father is making plans to marry."

Actually I burst into laughter. *My* father. As if he had not always been more hers and Josephine's father than anyone else's! But it was more than that. Father was a man of eighty-one, afflicted with the numerous ailments of old age. How was it possible not to be amused by the image of him as a bridegroom? Yet I knew my laughter was a rude and impolitic thing to do, and when my sister Josephine called a few minutes later I was well enough prepared to be able to restrain myself. The idea at the very first, however, struck me as funny on several levels. First, it was funny to me in view of the ridiculous picture of Father that Betsy and Jo had been painting of him in recent letters: Each had written me accounts of his two kinds of nightlife, his evenings with the old ladies and his nights on the town with the youngish women. (The letters had been intended certainly as humorous.) Second, there was the lifelong image I had had of Father *as* father, and *as* husband and *as* a man with such natural or assumed authority that his children could never even contemplate an important step like marriage without receiving *his* advice and consent—or, rather, without accepting his inevitable rejection of the loved one. None of his four children, you see, has ever married. And now here were his two unmarried, middle-aged daughters about to have the final word on his *own* marriage plans. I could not explain my amusement to Betsy. But when she did not join in with my laughter, I said: "And who's the unlucky girl?" It was the old ironic line any of us might have taken about Father at such a moment.

There was another silence, and then: "Phil, it's no joking matter. She's a Mrs. Clara Stockwell. She lives out toward Germantown, not very far from Mother's and Father's house." This was the first reference either sister had made to Mother in connection with Father's nightlife. And now somehow Betsy made it sound as though Mother were yet alive and perhaps living there in that sprawling one-story suburban house which Father had had built for their old age. The reference interested me mildly. It indicated, I thought, some new feeling coming into my sister's view of matters. But still I was not greatly concerned and still could not muster nearly so much interest as was expected of me, except of course I did think of the money. And I told myself that it was only Father's money that interested me. I told myself that perhaps I was beginning to understand what those other middle-aged sons and daughters of old Memphis widowers must have felt. So far as I knew his whole estate might someday go to his future wife. And what I seemed to understand least of all was what my own feelings would be in that case.

But certainly I was not scandalized by Father's behavior. I cast about for something pertinent on the subject that I might now say to Betsy. I am never very good on the telephone. Then presently Betsy said, as though the idea had just struck her: "These silences are expensive, Phillip." After that, she began urging the trip to Memphis on me. She said it was imperative that I come the very next day. And when my sister Josephine's call came, it was much the same. It was as though they had coordinated their efforts in advance. Their main point was to see that I was aboard the plane to Memphis next morning. From Jo's call, which came so soon after Betsy's that I was still sitting beside the telephone when it rang, I learned only that Mrs. Stockwell was, herself, going to join Jo and Betsy and Father for dinner at the Memphis Country Club that very night. And it seemed to me afterward that apparently a minor point of hers and Betsy's coordination had been to give me as little information as possible about Mrs. Clara Stockwell herself.

AFTER THE SECOND call was concluded I continued to sit for a long while beside the telephone in the loggia of my apartment. Total darkness had descended before I put on a light and went into my study. While I sat there I seemed to see my father at that very hour—it would have been an hour earlier in Memphis, of course—moving about the twilight shadows of his suburban house while simultaneously his two daughters, twenty blocks away, had been on the long-distance telephone with me, plotting the defeat of what must now be his great purpose in life. I think I felt totally indifferent. I thought only: Oh, the foolishness of Memphis ways! And I felt a surge of happiness that I had got away so long ago.

Yet I found myself longing to know something concrete about how the two women would proceed against the old man. Casting about in my mind, I began remembering the tribulations of the old widowers I had heard about when we first came to Memphis to live. The names of several such old men came readily to mind—their names and their various unhappy destinies. There was a Mr. Joel Manning, for instance. He was one of the earliest victims after I began to take notice of such histories. When Mr. Joel's intention to remarry was made manifest he was actually hauled into court by his own children. (His sons were all lawyers, unhappily for him.) And there in court, before all the world, so to speak, Mr. Joel's sons had their father declared non compos mentis. Those middle-aged lawyer sons were able to achieve this even though a host of Mr. Joel's lifelong friends testified, under oath, either that Mr. Joel Manning was perfectly sane or at least, as one of his oldest and most trusted friends phrased it, "as sane as he had ever been." (That, I am afraid, is how old friends are likely to serve one in moments of danger.)

You may say all this does not speak well for Memphis judicial processes, and yet that is not the whole of the matter. As I continued to sit by my telephone and as the twilight darkness continued to deepen, I found I was able to recall also the commanding figure of one Colonel Comus Fielding. When Colonel Fielding made known his own wishes to remarry, his three daughters, each the wife of a Memphis physician, caused their father to be confined to a private hospital, as such places were called in those days. And he was shut up there for the duration of his life. While in the private hospital, the Colonel, upon orders of his son-in-law doctors, of course, was permitted to receive male visitors only—not even old widows or spinsters from his immediate family. And what, I have to ask, does this say about the Memphis medical profession and its lofty ideals and processes?

As I continued sitting there by my telephone, in full darkness now, still one more example pressed itself upon my memory: the case of a certain Judge Joe Murray Gaston, long since
retired from the bench. At the remarkable age of ninety-six
Judge Gaston expressed the unheard-of desire to marry his
Yankee-Irish housekeeper, a woman who had been imported
from Boston to Memphis for the very purpose of looking
after him in his widowerhood. Immediately upon disclosure
of his wish and intention to marry this housekeeper, Judge
Gaston's children (all of them being well past sixty) forcibly
exiled the old nonagenarian to his own Mississippi cotton
farm, establishing him down there for his few remaining
years under the care of two rough field hands, constituting
his household staff in what was euphemistically referred to as
the "plantation manor house"—altogether beyond reach, of
course, of any female predator in Memphis.

THOUGH IT IS with present-day events in my family's
life that I am primarily concerned here, still certain events of
the past will have to be dredged up if present events are to be
fully comprehended. For instance, it will be necessary to say
something about my father's break with Mr. Lewis Shackleford, in Nashville, and to show something of that break's effect
upon my two sisters, as well as upon the lives of my mother
and my late brother, and ultimately even its effect upon my
own life with Holly Kaplan. And I cannot resist this opportunity to point out how the evil which men like Lewis
Shackleford do, men who have come to power either through
the use of military force or through preaching the Word of
God or through the manipulation of municipal bonds, as was
Mr. Shackleford's case, how the evil they do, that is to say,
has its effect finally not merely upon its immediate victims
(in the moment of killing or deceiving or cheating) but also

at last upon myriads of persons in all the millennia to come. By way of example, who could have thought that poor, dear Holly Kaplan, a Jewish girl from Cleveland, Ohio, and scarcely born into the world at the time of my family's flight from Nashville, could someday be affected by the misdeeds of Mr. Lewis Shackleford? If all this seems an unnecessary digression in these notes I am making on my family's life, at least it will give some idea of the passion I can be brought to feel even today by my own mention of Lewis Shackleford's name.

More than forty years ago, in 1931, my father, after his devastating reverses in Nashville, resolved, for better or worse, to pull up stakes there and remove his family and his law practice to Memphis. This would seem a small thing to someone not acquainted with distinctions made between the two cities in the minds of the local people there. Surely it *was* a small thing; yet for everyone in the Carver family, excepting possibly Father himself, the removal came at the worst possible age. Perhaps for Mother, who was past forty and had never lived outside the environs of Nashville, it had the worst effect of all, though certainly it did not seem so at the time. It was she who kept up the spirits of all the rest of us. With her ironic cast of mind and her sense and knowledge of local history she kept comparing our removal to the various events of early Tennessee history. We were like the Donelson party on the voyage down the Tennessee River, making their way through the flocks of swans at Moccasin Bend. We were like the Watauga men setting out for the Great Powwow on the Long Island of the Holston. Or what she liked best of all, we were like the Cherokees being driven from their ancestral lands on the notorious Trail of Tears.

Our removal proved to be a disaster for everyone except Father, I think. Somehow or other he managed successfully to establish his law practice in Memphis and to begin his professional life over in the very depths of the Great Depression. I think he may have managed it successfully because so many businessmen in Memphis knew how back in Nashville he had been deceived and cheated by the man he trusted and admired most in the world. There can be no question that a big part of the legal business that came to him in Memphis came from men who identified with him as another innocent, honest victim of Mr. Lewis Shackleford. Because Mr. Shackleford's financial empire extended far beyond the city limits of Nashville and, for that matter, far beyond the borders of Tennessee. Father's reputation as an honest man betrayed by a common enemy went before him and cannot have hurt him as a lawyer in Memphis. And what must have made him seem still more appealing was that he was generally known to be unwilling to discuss with anyone Lewis Shackleford's character or his infamous "gambling with other people's money." Such loyalty as Father displayed was to be valued in a lawyer, and perhaps his mere discretion even more so. He would soon acquire such an extensive practice in Memphis that he could scarcely have the time to look back on the old Nashville days of the twenties or reflect upon the injuries that had been done him by his friend there.

For the rest of us this time to look back was not lacking. Time hung heavy on our hands in our new Memphis abode. Certainly it did for Betsy and Josephine, who were then twenty and nineteen, respectively, and who since they had already been brought out as young ladies in Nashville society could not be presented in Memphis. Young ladies in present-day Memphis and Nashville cannot possibly conceive the profound significance that the debutante season once held for their like or imagine the strict rules that it was death to disobey. One absolutely inviolable rule was that a girl could be presented simultaneously in two cities but could not come out in different cities in successive years. And these were important matters for people like us in the place where we were. I suppose the reasoning was that otherwise some girl who had not found romance and marriage after a year of being "out" in Nashville might move on to Memphis the next year and New Orleans the next and possibly Louisville the next and after that even St. Louis and Washington, and so on as long as her matronly aunts and cousins lasted in those other cities and were willing to present her there. A girl could go on and on until her luck changed and at last she was chosen by some eligible young man. Clearly, as in any other game, this would be unfair, and it would have made the process of debutantism even more ridiculous than otherwise. The reasoning was, I suppose, you have your one chance and you take it.

Well, my sister Betsy and everyone around her thought her luck had been extremely good during her debutante year in Nashville. From the first ball of the season she was wooed by one Wyant Brawley. And by the time my younger sister Josephine had her own coming out, next year, Betsy and Wyant were treated practically as an engaged couple. But this was not put into words. Possibly Betsy and Wyant didn't make a formal announcement because they did not wish to draw any attention from Jo's debut. The two girls were very considerate of each other and perhaps the more so because in those days they seemed so very different in character and appearance. Betsy was blonde and vivacious, an excellent horsewoman, was even a good jumper, and was good at all the outdoor sports. Jo was dark-haired and blue-eyed and much more striking-looking than Betsy. I won't say she was intellectual but she was more introspective than her older sister and attracted young men of a different kind. It was only after we were in Memphis that they began to seem so much alike. By the time I was receiving letters from them off in New York, fifteen years later, their handwritings were almost identical, and I would have to turn a letter over and see the name on the reverse side in order to know whom it was from. They made a great point in those later days of their individuality and of their independence from each other, but I often suspected they did so because they were aware of the ever-increasing likeness between them. I believe also that Betsy and Wyant meant to wait until Wyant had finished medical school before marrying. Wyant was considered by everyone an immensely eligible suitor. He was descended from two of Nashville's most distinguished families. He was one of the heirs presumptive to the well-known Wyant estate. He was a graduate of Wallace Preparatory School. Like my father he was a former star of the Vanderbilt squad. And he was a member of the Phi Delta Theta fraternity, which was wonderfully important in Nashville.

Even so, in the months before the removal to Memphis the usually extraverted Betsy would often be found alone in a downstairs room gazing out the window despondently. Or we would see her walking aimlessly about the lawn, obviously wishing to be out there alone with her thoughts. Perhaps she *was* "only thinking," as she would say if her younger brother asked her what she was doing by the window or out on the lawn. But finally my mother called the four children together one day and made us a little speech, which I am sure was intended primarily for Betsy's ears. Mother reminded us of the ugly and near-ruinous ordeal that Father had just been through with Lewis Shackleford and told us that we must not in any way resent the imminent move to Memphis and that we must not, above all, allow Father to feel that we were grieving about leaving Nashville or brooding about the changes to come in our lives. I recall that I almost shouted out then in my thirteen-year-old-boy innocence that, anyway, we'd *all* be coming back to Nashville to visit and that Betsy would very soon be coming back to live. But something about the expression in Mother's hazel eyes, now suddenly fixed on me, warned me not to say it. In retrospect, it seems to me that until the day we left Nashville my mother knew by instinct or by training how to deal with every problem or situation that arose in our family. She knew her role in the family unit so well that she never had any doubt what her behavior should be. But from the day we arrived in Memphis it seemed she never under any circumstances had any sense of what was fitting or any feeling of responsibility with regard to the role of a mother in an old-fashioned family like ours. She continued to be affectionate with each of us individually but any idea of the family or of herself as mother seemed as meaningless to her as all the silly debutantism that her daughters had to go through and the life in the business world that Father was caught up in. It may be that by that time—1931—the family in our sort of world and in our part of the country, without any real economic function or any relation to the old earth it had been formed by or any significance in the heavens above, was now such a frail and fractious thing that even so slight a shift as from one Southern city to another (with their almost imperceptible difference—laughably alike they would seem to an outsider) could destroy all balance, poise, health that it had to have in order to survive. Certainly our Memphis move's coming just when it did increased the shattering impact. For my two sisters it would ultimately have the effect of freezing them in the roles of eternal young ladies. (Even after they were corpulent and wrinkled middle-aged personages they frequently appeared in dresses that should have been worn only by young girls.) For me and my brother the effect was possibly still worse. For my brother I think it meant his early death in the War. (He pretended he was drafted, though actually he volunteered to serve with the Air Corps and was killed on D-Day, flying as part of the first cover for the landing.) For me it meant something not altogether unlike that, though not so easily recognized. For

Mother it meant a total alteration of her role within our family and at the same time a kind of personal liberation for which she was not prepared and of which she did not know how to make an advantage. Perhaps, though, it wasn't the move at all. Perhaps we were something vestigial—as a family, as a class of people even. Perhaps it wasn't the move but only my father's insistence that the family should be moved intact, merely an expression of his need to have his wife and children with him, and with himself altogether unchanged, if he were to successfully begin his career over like a young man.

2

MY MOTHER HAD been born and bred in Nashville. She was the product of a rather formal, old society which she had grown up in there and indirectly the product of the Richmond world *her* mother had come out of. As a girl and as a young wife and mother she had been guided by the old rules and by the firm hand of her own mother, who died only a few months before we left Nashville. But it wasn't really Mother's nature to become the formal sort of person that Richmond and Nashville had made her. There were times even in Nashville when she said genuinely witty and even risqué things, which none of us was quite prepared for. She said once, before a roomful of people, that any gin drink made her see double and feel single. My grandmother commented on that occasion that Mother tended to be an overly witty "young girl," verging sometimes on silliness, sometimes on the obscene. Grandmother said she didn't know what might have become of Mother in this life if she had not happened to be well born and well bred. But mostly I remember

Mother in Nashville after Father and Mr. Shackleford had broken off and as she was that day when she called her four children to her and instructed us not to let Father see us if and when we moped about the coming removal to Memphis. That was the day when she said she feared our move was going to be like the Cherokees' Trail of Tears.

Nowadays it seems strange to have once lived in a Nashville where phrases like "well bred" and "well born" were always ringing in one's ears and where distinctions between "genteel people" and "plain people" were made and where there was rather constant talk about who was a gentleman and who wasn't a gentleman. When I am back in Nashville now on some publishing business or other, the city seems to me—me, the outsider—just like any other post–World War II city, as much like Columbus, Ohio, as like Richmond, Virginia. I often have to remind myself where I really am. Staying at the downtown Hyatt Regency, I have to remind myself that this is where the old Polk Apartments once stood and where still earlier stood the imposing residence of Mrs. James K. Polk, Nashville's social arbiter for half a century. Or if in very recent years I am staying in Memphis and I happen to put up at the midtown Holiday Inn, I have to make a point of recalling the fine residences that once stood on that site. Yet there is a difference between these two provincial cities even nowadays. Each has its nucleus of high rises at the center and its spreading suburbs for miles around, but still there *is* a difference between them. And it's not just its old money and its country music that makes Nashville different from Memphis. Even with its present-day vulgar, ugly, plastic look and sound there is a little something else left for anyone who was once under Nashville's spell. As one walks or rides down any street in Nashville one can feel now and again that he has just glimpsed some pedestrian on the sidewalk who was not quite real somehow, who with a glance over his shoulder or with a look in his disenchanted eye has warned one not to believe too much in the plastic present and has given warning that the past is still real and present somehow and is demanding something of all men like me who happen to pass that way. I don't know what all this represents precisely. It seems to say something to me not about all that I remember of my Nashville childhood but about all that I have forgotten, all that the Merciful Censor has blotted from my memory. My mother used to tell us that Nashville was fought for against the Indians by the early white settlers and that it was the spirit of the slaughtered Indians hovering over the place that made everybody there so queer. Then she would laugh and say that on the other hand Memphis didn't have any such spirits, Memphis didn't in effect have any soul or any real history. Memphis was a place that had simply been laid out and sold off like any other town. She said she didn't, herself, mind that but that it was a prejudice Father could never quite overcome.

And when I heard my mother saying such fanciful things I would wonder why our family was so much concerned with the likes of that and concerned with how and where it was we lived. It was only after Mother was dead and my sisters finally began trying to prevent Father's remarrying that I conceived the notion that we were somehow like the families of those other old men who had suffered at the hands of their grown-up, middle-aged children. Perhaps with our strong sense of who we were and where we had come from we really were, as I have already suggested, somehow vestigial in these latter days and were ourselves deviants in some evolutionary progress.

After we moved to Memphis I don't recall Mother's ever once saying: "A gentleman must always" do so and so. Or: "A lady will never" do so and so. She no longer quoted her mother to us. She no longer said the things she and we thought were expected of her. The old delicate balance between her wild nature and her strict, Presbyterian, genteel upbringing was gone in Memphis. For the short time that she kept her health it seemed that she was going to develop an entirely new personality, despite Father's rather constant effort to restrain her and remind her of what she was "really like." During this short period she spoke nearly always for the sake of amusing herself and amusing others. At times when the whole family would seem to be in a state of depression she would say: "If somebody doesn't say something cheerful, I'm going to go out and jump in the Mississippi River. That swirling muddy water in my ears would be more cheering than this silence." Or when we were all in the doldrums she more than once said: "I sometimes think a shooting in the family would have been better than a move to Memphis." At the time I wondered if she meant what I thought she meant. In Nashville one had been always hearing about the old duels fought by men like Jackson and Dickinson, of the Cooper-Carmack shooting that divided the great families of the town forever, and of how at a meeting of the board of directors of one bank, the retiring—or ousted—chairman had reached behind the door, brought forth a shotgun, and had taken aim and shot the incoming chairman, firing down the full length of the board of directors' table. Perhaps that was a side of Nashville life that Mother hated most to leave.

I had already found myself speculating, before that day even—usually after I was in bed at night—about what the result might have been if Father had gone out and shot Mr. Lewis Shackleford instead of carting us off to Memphis. *Then* he certainly would not have had to live in the same town with the villain, and I would not have had to leave Mr. Wallace's school or leave the little girl with the dark eyes and the Dutch bob or my horse Red that I had just now got over being afraid of. But whenever Mother said that about shooting,

Father would presently show signs of an attack of indigestion or find some other excuse to absent himself from the room. And if we then chided Mother—ever so gently—for the suggestion (suppressing, of course, our real thoughts on the subject—the wish that Father *had* shot Mr. S.) she would only laugh and say: "I was only joking, of course." And presently she would add: "In adversity you have to learn to live off your sense of humor. As you well know, I like Memphis a whale of a lot better than any of you do. It just suits *me*. I'll be happy to live and die in Memphis." And sometimes she liked to tell the story of what some old Nashville lady—some friend of her mother's—had said to her when she was contemplating the move to Memphis.

"Nashville," the old woman had said, "is a city of schools and churches, whereas Memphis is—well, Memphis is something else again. Memphis is a place of steamboats and cotton gins, of card playing and hotel society. Anyway," the woman went on to say to Mother, "*you*, my dear Minta, will *love* Memphis." As a matter of fact, I believe Mother did instantly love Memphis and but for Father would have melted into the life there. She liked cards and gossip and striking clothes and Country Club food. During her first months there she took to using the slang of the period and assumed Memphis's own way of putting things. About a new dress she had bought, the waist of which Betsy said was a bad length for Mother's short figure, Mother declared: "I don't care whether it becomes my figure or not. I just want to know if it looks the latest fashion." And when she was going to a big Memphis party where there would be mostly people she had not met before, she insisted to Father: "I don't want to make merely a good impression. I want to make a killing. What else is there to go to a party full of new people for?"

All in all, she preferred her new life or would have preferred it if Father had allowed her to, preferred it to the old days of fox hunting and horse shows in the Nashville basin and hunt breakfasts at some antebellum mansion out on Franklin Pike ("all that Nashville stuff") or at steeplechase weekends up in Sumner County, liked it better than musical afternoons at the Nashville Centennial Club or serious literary evenings centered on some professor from Vanderbilt (with his reconstructed views on the advancing South) or formal dinner parties with the women going upstairs after dinner. That had been *her* Nashville, *our* Nashville. Memphis was something else. It was all card parties for the women and golf for the men. Memphis was today. Nashville was yesterday. Mother was willing to forget Nashville. Father wished to live Nashville in Memphis.

That is how our parents' new life seemed to us children. Perhaps we weren't the best judges, but we could see, anyway, our parents' marriage was different from before. Maybe it was just a coincidence that their marriage had gone into a new phase at that crucial time—that is, when we moved. Maybe Mother didn't care about sex any longer. Maybe Father didn't. That's how one would speculate nowadays, though of course not in those days. At any rate, I am confident there was no extramarital love affair on the part of either. But from the day we arrived in Memphis, Mother was busy with new women friends all day, and Father was occupied at his office, working as he probably had not worked since he was a very young man, trying to establish the new law practice during those lean Depression years.

Yes, perhaps it was only that their time of life coincided with the changed circumstances. Nevertheless, to us children some alteration in their pattern of life together was apparent. I was thirteen. My brother was fifteen. My sisters were nine-teen and twenty. We were old enough and idle enough to observe that there was some difference in the marriage. Mainly we saw Mother devoting herself to a new kind of social life amongst women, a kind she had never had before. And then one morning she woke with a strange headache in her right temple. She had Father bring her the morning paper and asked the cook to bring her coffee and toast in bed. For thirty years afterward she seldom got into her daytime clothes, even working in the garden sometimes in her nightgown and housecoat.

THE DAY WE had set out for Memphis from Nashville, my sister Betsy's fiancé, Wyant Brawley, was on hand. It had been decided that Wyant would come along—just for the ride—in his own car. Betsy of course rode with him. In his Nash convertible also would ride Josephine's bulldog and the family cat, the two of which were good enough friends to make the journey together. In Mother's sedan—"the Chrysler," it was always so referred to—would ride Jo, my brother Georgie, and I in the back seat, with the family chauffeur and houseman of that period—Mac, that is—at the steering wheel, and between him and his wife, Mildred, being the cook and maid of course, was Father's favorite setter, Buck. (Father had given away his other setter and sold his three valuable pointers, as well as four foxhounds, in preparation for this move, which came in the very worst days of the Great Depression. He had also divested himself of his two jumpers, a gaited mare that really had belonged to Mother, my own horse Red, my brother's aging polo pony, and two spotted ponies left over from our childhood days.) In "the Packard," as Father's car was always designated, was Father at the wheel and Mother beside him and, in the back seat, there was Harriet, who doubled as upstairs maid and laundress, sitting between the two cages that contained Mother's canary bird and Betsy's pair of lovebirds. Our procession set out at nine in the morning, well organized by Father. He had arranged that packers and movers be there the day before and that they get everything into the van except the beds we slept in. Then on the morning of departure for Memphis they threw in the beds, and we were off.

Father gave the vans half an hour's start on us, whether for style or for convenience on the road I do not know. But after the movers were gone I remember our standing about the empty house. I think that in a sense Mother had not acknowledged to herself that we were really leaving. The packing up, and all that, must have seemed like some kind of make-believe game to her who had never in her life, except for a short stay at Thornton, lived anywhere but Nashville. But now she moved about the empty house with an air of authority, inspecting the rooms for any uncleaned corner. It was with her old, Nashville air of authority that we would seldom see again after we got to Memphis. I recall she even examined the windowsills for dust and ran her white-gloved forefinger along one mantel shelf, the way her mother had used to do. It was not until she was in the car and we were all about ready to venture forth that she seemed to understand the finality of the moment. She was seated in the front seat of the Packard when Father got into the driver's seat and closed the car door. Suddenly at that moment, when he firmly closed his door, she broke into deep sobbing and for several moments wept uncontrollably. We all crowded around the car, the four grown-up or nearly grown-up children and the three black servants. Father took her into his arms, and I shall always have the feeling, though of course I do not think it literally true, that it was the last time he ever took her in his arms. Then just as suddenly as she had begun, she ceased her weeping. With her eyes still teary she smiled and said that she did not wish to leave a trail of tears. And she said to us that it was the thought of leaving her "little house" and garden that had upset her. She had lived there for more than twenty years, excepting the year when Father's father had died and we went and stayed with him in his house at Thornton while he was dying. She didn't mention leaving Nashville itself. She was thinking of Father's feelings, I believe, and so she spared him any such reference. She had passed her infancy, her childhood, her young ladyhood, her young married years, the whole of her life until then in Nashville, but she mentioned only leaving the house, which represented the life she and Father had had together.

During that last thirty minutes after the vans had set out, when most of us stood in a doorway or leaned against a bare wall or wandered aimlessly about from room to room, Father had made inspections of his own—of the house and the outbuildings. Our house was actually four miles south of town and was situated on a hilltop in the center of a small estate, which on one side adjoined the very large estate and horse farm of Mr. Lewis Shackleford. Father's inspection did not consist of taking one long last look at the house and stables where he had enjoyed life for the past twenty years or taking one last glance across the little valley to where Mr. Shackleford's great replica of a Georgian mansion stood and where Father and Mother had been so frequently entertained, year after year. His inspection had but one purpose: to make certain that not a single possession of his or even any rubbish or sweepings from the house had been left behind. The place had not yet been sold, but a sign would go up at the front gate next day, offering it for sale. He was making a clean sweep. When finally he joined the rest of us on the front porch and indicated that we should now get into the cars and set out for Memphis, he said, more to himself than to us: "Well, we have left nothing behind. We have everything that's ours. Now let's go." He meant chiefly, I think now, that *he* had *us*. No doubt it was upon hearing him say what he did, and understanding it better than the rest of us at the time, that Mother imagined that in his eyes we were primarily his chattels. Perhaps it was that more than the way he closed the car door that caused her presently to burst into tears.

By lunchtime our party had crossed the Tennessee River and arrived at the town of Huntingdon. We stopped there for lunch in the old hotel on the square. My father had, himself, come originally of course from West Tennessee, and when we got out of the cars at Huntingdon I could feel his spirits beginning to soar—just because we had now crossed into the country of his own boyhood, where he had lived before he ever knew Lewis Shackleford. He had come to Nashville first as a college freshman, at the turn of the century. He did well in his studies at Vanderbilt and had played left end on the football squad. The fact was, he was named all-Southern end in 1902 and became such a hero to Nashville boys somewhat younger than himself that he could not stroll down West End Avenue without being followed by a cluster of Nashville boys like little Lewis Shackleford. I have heard him speak many times of his own impressions of Nashville when he first went there from the little county seat of Thornton, out in the West Tennessee cotton country, where his father and grandfather had been lawyers and landowners. He would talk about what elegant people in those days still lived in the old mansions along West End and on Eighth Avenue, in Nashville.

It was in one of those houses on West End Avenue that my mother had been a girl, and it was there that he met and courted her. The Vanderbilt boys would go calling in veritable throngs, on Sunday afternoons, at the houses where such girls lived. He and she fell to talking at one such Sunday gathering, he standing with his elbow resting on the high mantel shelf in her mother's parlor, she from her diminutive height looking up into his blue eyes that seemed, underneath his shock of black hair, to express some ideal of honor and truth itself. After his undergraduate years he stayed on at Vanderbilt to

study law, and my mother, by then regularly receiving his
Sunday-afternoon calls, waited patiently till he had finished
law school and had got himself established in a practice there
in Nashville. Then they were married. I think they very soon
became—Father with his remarkable energy and lively intelligence and Mother with her seeming balance of vivacity and
propriety—one of the most admired and sought-after couples
on that old-fashioned social scene.

In the dining room of the big clapboard hotel at Huntingdon, scarcely forty miles from where he was born and bred,
Father grew very expansive. He knew the owner of the hotel,
as well as the clerk at the desk. They both were natives of
his own Thorn County. It was the last week in September,
and he discussed the crops with them and had something to
say about West Tennessee politics. In the dining room Betsy
and Wyant, quite by accident, met up with some young people from Nashville who were visiting a Vanderbilt classmate
in Huntingdon. They decided to sit at the table with them.
Father clearly disapproved of their doing so but he said nothing directly about it. He went on talking to the innkeeper,
who had now seated himself at our table. But from time to
time I would see Father glancing uneasily at the young people
at the other table across the room. When we got up to leave,
he made a signal to Betsy that said we were ready to set out.
Presently Betsy rose and came over alone to where we were
all standing near the cash register at the front counter. As she
crossed the splintery dining-room floor, in her high heels, I
remember how her long bob of blonde hair tossed about at-
tractively and I remember the broad, questioning smile she
wore. I thought she was beautiful, and she looked very happy.
And one could see Wyant Brawley back at the young people's table, keeping his eyes trained on her. Father, unsmiling,
watched her as she approached as though he knew she was
to be the bearer of bad news. All she said was that she and

Wyant wished to talk a few minutes longer with their friends. They would follow in a few minutes. Father said nothing. Mother smiled and said: "Don't get lost." Betsy said Wyant knew the road. And then she went back to the other table.

Bouncing along the rough macadam highway, after we had got deeper into the cotton country, Father kept periodically slowing the car down. In the back seat of Mother's sedan, Josephine and Georgie and I could tell by the angle of his head, underneath his broad-brimmed straw hat, that he was looking in the rearview mirror, trying to see if Wyant's car had come in sight. At the mill town of Huxley, where we stopped for gas, Betsy and Wyant still had not made an appearance. As we pulled into the service station there, I saw Father spring out of the Packard onto the pavement, his face red, his straw hat now pulled down over his eyes. Then I saw him hurrying inside the service station, where he asked to use the telephone. Josephine and Georgie and I went over to Mother's car window. She told us Father was telephoning back to Huntingdon to see if Betsy and Wyant had left. Mother wore a very long face. She looked as if she might have been crying. "He has taken the absurd notion," she began, and then she burst not into tears but into a kind of hysterical, girlish laughter that I don't recall ever before that day having heard from her but which I would hear many times afterward. This laughter would come always on those occasions when the unhappiness of her children in their new life in Memphis would suddenly seem to her what she described as "too absurd to be ridiculous" and when she therefore felt that she could no longer help or even sympathize with us. "He has taken the absurd notion," she said through her laughter, "that Wyant and Betsy have turned back to Nashville and intend to be married there—right away, and not follow us to Memphis!" I remember that my sister Josephine's face, at this point, turned ashen. I can only suppose that she saw herself abandoned by Betsy, saw herself going into the new Memphis life alone, so to speak. My own thought was—though I would never have admitted it to anyone: Why in the world should Wyant and Betsy not have turned back and why should Betsy come to Memphis at all? Then I saw Father emerge from the service station office, looking quite as ashen as Josephine had looked. (They had the same coloring, but they were of such different temperaments that one rarely noticed the fact except in moments like this one when they were showing some deep emotion.) We all watched him as he approached the car where we were gathered, and as he subsequently stuck his head in through the front window on the driver's side. "They left Huntingdon soon after we did," he said through his teeth, and he looked through the car, across Mother, at Jo and Georgie and me, looked at us accusingly as though he were sure we had been conspirators in an elopement plot.

But at that moment Wyant's Nash convertible appeared on the macadam road and presently turned off the highway and into the service station. Mother said: "Don't say anything to Wyant and Betsy about telephoning back!" Father immediately withdrew his head. Presently he was talking to the attendant about filling the tanks of our two cars with gas. He didn't once look in Betsy and Wyant's direction. While the gas tanks were being filled, I observed that the chauffeur and the cook and the maid had got out of the cars and had gone to stand at the curb near the roadside. They were speaking softly amongst themselves and were pointing off across the cotton fields that began there on the outskirts of Huxley. This town of Huxley was only a dozen miles or so from the old county seat of Thornton, where Father had been born and where these Negro servants had been born, too. A number of years before, Father had brought them all to Nashville

to work for us, just as he had persuaded other Thornton Negroes to come to Nashville and work for his friend Lewis
Shackleford. Father now looked at the group standing on the
distant curb, pointing off in the direction of their and his
hometown. Still watching them, he took off his big straw hat
and wiped his brow with his white handkerchief. The fact
was, just after Lewis Shackleford had betrayed him—when
he first learned of the betrayal—and before he decided to
move us to Memphis there had been a period when he seriously considered taking all of us to Thornton to live in his old
family place. I think this was a great temptation to him, after
his humiliation in Nashville, to go back to Thornton and take
up the practice of law in his father's old shotgun office on the
town square. Such a retreat from the world would certainly
have been much easier than beginning his career over in the
relatively high-powered competition of Memphis. Of course
he finally made his firm decision to go to Memphis, but
Mother told me long after the day of the move that when it
had got to be midafternoon and we had got no farther on our
way to Memphis than Huxley, and with Father already seeming quite tired, she suggested that we drive the twelve miles
over to Thornton and spend the night in the family home-
place there. She said he lost his temper with her because of
that suggestion and accused her of thinking he was a man who
did not know his own mind. Yet in the first moments after he
drove the long Packard automobile into the Huxley service
station, before he had turned off the ignition even or opened
the door to spring out onto the pavement, he had said to
Mother: "I do think maybe we should spend the night in
Thornton, after all."

I suspect that if Betsy and Wyant had not turned up and
we had gone to Thornton for the night Father would never
have left there and would never have set up his practice and

his new life in Memphis at all. But after the arrival of Betsy and Wyant I suspect he experienced a moment of fright at the thought of what he had contemplated doing—that is, giving up and going back to Thornton. And it was as though when he saw the servants standing over at the roadside and pointing excitedly off toward Thornton he felt he knew exactly what was on their mind. Suddenly he called out to them: "You people get back in the cars! We're about to be on our way!" It was a sort of command I had seldom if ever before heard him give to servants. It really was as though he did that because we were now in West Tennessee, which is more like the Deep South. It was as though the servants were family slaves, like their forebears, and he had caught them on the verge of making a dash for freedom or possibly, as it may have seemed momentarily, of making an escape back into the safe old days of slavery at Thornton. During those dark days of the Depression I think many people had such fantasies. But maybe it was only that Father was thinking that he *must* arrive in Memphis with the entire family household intact if he was to make a new go of things. I think possibly he felt that was the only way he could endure this transition. He could only have the strength to start over if he felt he had lost nothing of himself, if he was certain that all his dependents were still his dependents. No one must be allowed to defect or he would feel that he was not entering whole into the life ahead of him. Something like that, I think. He did enter so, and perhaps that *is* what sustained him in the years immediately afterward, sustained *him* and in some degree destroyed the rest of us. Once we had left Huxley that afternoon, once we had *not* gone over to Thornton for the night, once the caravan had headed on to Memphis, as Mother reported to us afterward, his spirits began to rise and continued to rise with every mile until by the time we drove up to the house he had leased on Stonewall Place, out there in Memphis, he was actually whistling "Home, Sweet Home" and waving out the car window to those of us riding in the second car.

WITHIN SIX WEEKS after we arrived on Stonewall Place, whatever understanding had existed between Betsy and Wyant was broken off. Wyant had come for visits on two weekends. On each occasion, as during the two days he remained with us after the day we arrived, Father could hardly be brought to speak to him. And he did not speak to Betsy for several days following each visit. When he came home at night from his new Memphis office he went about the house with the air of a wounded animal and seemed suspicious of all four of us children. It was as though during that painful period when Wyant and Betsy had lagged behind on the road to Huxley, Father had cast Wyant Brawley forever into outer darkness. Or maybe it had happened at the moment when Wyant had led Betsy off to sit at the table with the Nashville young people in the Huntingdon hotel dining room. Toward the end of the second weekend visit Wyant finally came to Father and asked him just what he had done to give offense. His presuming to question Father about this was perhaps the real beginning of the end for him and Betsy. She did not want Wyant to go to Father with such a question. It was too likely to be upsetting to him, and all four of us children had by now come to feel without being reminded by Mother that our father was entitled to have peace of mind in his own house. I don't think Betsy ever forgave Wyant for going to Father that last afternoon or that Wyant forgave her for asking him not to do so. They corresponded during several months afterward, and Betsy accepted an invitation for a four-day visit at the Brawleys' house in Nashville, though she did not stay for the full four days. On the third day, Josephine telephoned her and told her that Father was in such a state that she thought Betsy ought to come home.

Betsy of course came. And when she got home she and Father had a talk that settled the whole matter once and for all. But during the interview on that last Saturday afternoon of Wyant's final visit, nothing had got settled, and Wyant had got no satisfaction from the answers Father gave him. Father had said merely that he had come to realize that Wyant could not be trusted. He was not trustworthy. But the answer had not of course sufficed for Wyant. Was it all because he had fallen a few miles behind that day on the road from Huntingdon to Huxley? No, it was not, Father had assured him. And all the rest of us in the rest of the house had heard Wyant's voice asking: "Then why not? Why shouldn't we marry? Why not? I demand to know why not!"

No matter what the circumstances, I believe we all resented anyone's speaking that way to Father. I don't know for certain of course how the others felt, but I went off and put my hands over my ears. It seemed the end of the world for someone to be speaking to my father like that. And a few weeks later when Betsy insisted on going off for that four-day visit with the Brawleys in Nashville we thought the house would come down about our heads. We could hear Father and Mother off in her room, raising *their* voices. Father had refused to give Betsy the money for the trip. Mother had supplied the money. She ended by apologizing for that, though, and saying it had been very wrong of her to do so. Then for a day there was a calm that turned into a terrible silence on Father's part, one which was beyond our endurance. When Betsy returned home a day early he received her with open arms and asked her to come into the sun parlor for that fateful talk of theirs. That was when he convinced her. She looked at him unflinchingly at first and then, according to her account, told him that he must not try to make her decision for her. He began by saying he had no power over her to do that, no power over her or her sister to tell them whom to marry or not marry. She didn't imagine, did she, that a father's authority was what it once had been?

Yet of course he had every power that such a man could have over such young women. A father with his personal charm, with his youthful physique, with his ocean-blue eyes, with his heavy head of coal-black hair still possessed a power over his daughters that was beyond all traditional parental power that fathers of earlier generations possessed. My sisters were not actually in love with him of course, and yet how could they know how to resist his power? I think he must, moreover, have resorted to every device he knew as a courtroom lawyer to win his case. But no doubt the final and most telling device was the charming description he gave Betsy of Wyant's person and character before then turning about and destroying his creation. In the end, he could give no proof of Wyant's untrustworthiness, of the likeliness, that is, of his someday deceiving and abandoning her. He insisted to her that *he* knew Nashville men, even that *he* knew in detail what an unfaithful husband Wyant's father had been to Wyant's mother. But he undoubtedly counted on Betsy's knowledge of whatever the weaknesses of Wyant's character may have been and counted on her own observations (or merely the natural suspicions of a lover) of indications that had already begun or of just how he might someday be unfaithful to her. In preparation for that psychological effect, however, he had presented to her such an attractive picture of Wyant as he ostensibly saw him, so accurate a picture, that is, as she herself actually saw Wyant, that Betsy could have no doubt that her father understood precisely what her feelings were for Wyant Brawley. His admiring, loving description of Wyant was such that one could almost have imagined that it was he, not his daughter, who possessed a romantic affection for the young man. It was clearly an inspired piece of work, this description of his of Wyant Brawley's attractive physical bearing, of his good manners, of his considerable intelligence. But even Betsy in her wretched emotional state could recognize that it was a work of her father's imagination, that the feelings were vicarious and not in the most usual sense romantic, and that the qualities attributed to Wyant Brawley were ones which her father once would have attributed to Mr. Lewis Shackleford. At any rate, Betsy now had no doubt that her father saw Wyant's good qualities as she saw them herself, and like the rest of us she had never really doubted Father's astute judgment of human character. And when in his peroration he brought forth the likelihood of Wyant's being a deceiver, his argument had been well prepared to convince. And no doubt Betsy, with the natural doubts and suspicions of a lover, was able to supply sufficient evidence to support his argument.

Her correspondence with Wyant continued for a while. But as Father would sometimes coyly point out, she was also in correspondence with several other young men in Nashville. Her engagement had not been so definite a thing as absolutely to preclude that. And soon there were weekend visits from at least three of these other suitors. But if one of them suggested coming a second time, Father said there was no point in such a visit. He told Betsy that she ought to begin making friends where she lived, ought to have her Junior League membership moved to Memphis.

MY SISTER JOSEPHINE had been so depressed on the day of our move from Nashville that as we rode together in the back seat of the Chrysler, she poured out her sorrows to me. It seemed to her that Betsy had all the luck in life. Betsy's debut year had been a great success and had ended with her engagement to Wyant Brawley, whereas in Jo's own year there had been no very attractive and eligible young men. At the end of her season there was still no one on the horizon whom she would for a moment consider marrying. She had a very different temperament from Betsy and always underestimated her own attractiveness and undervalued the people who admired her. With her dark hair and blue eyes she was actually better-looking than Betsy and had a warmth in her manner that made people respond to her every mood. If there was no appropriate suitor for her hand in matrimony during the year she came out, it was because most of the young men who went to Nashville debut parties were still too boyish to appreciate her particular kind of beauty and did not quite know what to make of the way her usually serene and dignified demeanor and her sometimes melancholy expression would suddenly vanish behind an explosive new mood or feeling, a burst of laughter, an almost rowdy talkativeness, even an expressive gesturing with her prettily formed hands that seemed an extension of her words. And it was this very trait in her personality that would within a year or so cause the somewhat older young men she met in Memphis to find her irresistibly attractive and to move at least a half dozen of them to make proposals of marriage. Within only a few months after her arrival, both she and Betsy were doing good works for "the League." It was while doing those good works for that highbrow organization that she met most of the Memphis "second-year girls," and it was through *them* of course that she met the eligible young men. One would have supposed those developments would have met with Father's immediate approval—and certainly with Mother's. But somehow they both seemed to feel that Josephine was moving in or settling in too fast in Memphis—something like that. Mother had become completely dependent upon Father for every opinion she expressed. Perhaps they felt Jo was forgetting Nashville too easily. Their resentment of her newfound popularity was expressed in such subtle and indirect ways that one could not really understand the nature of it. The fact was, for all Mother's liking for Memphis she was forever, with Father's encouragement, making fun of its institutions—of the Cotton Carnival, of Beale Street music, even of Boss Crump. And Father was always comparing something in Memphis unfavorably with something in Nashville, be it the Country Club or the railway station. For the most part, it was not actually something he said directly but something in the tone of his voice. And he spoke belittlingly of any young man who began coming to see Josephine. They somehow seemed smaller than Nashville young men, he said, and they seemed uncertain of their manners. Though Memphis was a considerably larger city than Nashville, the young men seemed countrier to him —more Mississippian it was, of course. Nashville was, by the Huntingdon–Huxley road, approximately two hundred twenty miles east of Memphis, two hundred twenty miles nearer to Richmond, to Charleston, to Savannah. But when Father spoke, one felt that it was more like two hundred twenty thousand miles.

At last Josephine singled out one of those young Memphians. Or one of them singled her out. His name was Clarkson Manning, and though it isn't particularly significant, I think he was the great-nephew of old Mr. Joel Manning. He had a good job at Union Planters Bank. (Father found the name of that bank rather amusing. Another beau of Josephine's worked on the newspaper, *The Commercial Appeal*, which name Father found a particularly comical name for a newspaper in a city of the old Confederacy.) Clarkson Manning was invited to dinner with the family a number of times. He was thought a very nice young man, even if he was a little bit too Mississippi Delta in his manners. In Father's books it was as bad to have the low-bowing, hat-removing manners and the ingratiating accent of the Mississippi Delta as it was to roll your *r*'s and have the ramrod, handshaking, hat-on-head manners of East Tennessee. Though he himself was born and bred at Thornton, on the banks of the muddy Forked Deer River, in the heart of West Tennessee, he judged all things by Middle Tennessee and Nashville, where he had had his successes in his profession and in his courtship and in his marriage.

Before dinner one night, this Clarkson Manning had an extra highball with Father, perhaps at Father's special urging. Possibly that drink loosed his tongue, or perhaps he had not been told by Josephine that a certain name was never mentioned in our house. At any rate, in giving an account of his own parents' romantic courtship (his parents were considerably older than our parents, and the two couples were not acquainted)—in giving this account, he mentioned in passing that his mother was the second cousin of Mr. Lewis Shackleford of Nashville. After he had spoken that name there was not a sound from anyone else at the table. But the faces all around must have changed. And possibly Clarkson *had* felt himself guilty of dropping the name of an important connection. Because his eyes did seem to go round the table, and he undoubtedly observed the changed look on our faces. His account stopped then and there. I thought the silence that followed would go on forever. Finally it was, to my consternation, Father who did speak. "And is your mother on good terms nowadays," he asked, "with her cousin—with *your* cousin?"

"Oh," said Clarkson Manning in the most ingenuous and self-congratulating tones, "she happens to be in Nashville now, visiting the Shacklefords." At the second mention of that name, Father trained his eyes on Mother at the other end of the table. Presently he said to her that he was not feeling well and that she must excuse him from the room. I think now he was not merely making an excuse, though I thought most certainly he was at the time. And I hated him for it. Later I would learn (through my own most difficult experience with him) that he *could* be made physically sick by a reference to his total withdrawal from his old life in Nashville. And "total withdrawal" of course meant the withdrawal of his total family.

Mother followed Father from the room—really for the sake of propriety, I think—and presently she returned, explaining to Clarkson that Father was given to having nervous-stomach upsets and that "you could never tell when such an upset might come on." It had nothing to do with anything of the moment at hand. Her explanation was of course wholly inadequate, but Mother had the air of not caring whether or not it was adequate, as indeed she didn't care. She had the air of only wishing to get through the moment and to forget it. With her somehow it was nowadays always a matter of merely getting through difficult moments in the family, not of dealing with them. . . . And of course within a matter of days my sister Josephine and Clarkson Manning had entirely broken off their romance.

M Y S I S T E R B E T S Y was by now drinking too much at the parties she went to in Memphis. When she came in at night she would wake the whole house with too loud talk and laughter. (Though she did not become an alcoholic and gave up drinking altogether after a year or so when her real estate business began to occupy her and consume the whole of her interest in life, I cannot help feeling nowadays that it might have been better if she had gone on drinking until there had been some sort of crisis about it. I think that might somehow have solved something for all of us.) As for me, I was by that time in a phase of surliness and of rebellious feeling against my father, though never showing my feelings directly to him. Even before we left Nashville I had been in love with a number of little girls whom I met at horse shows and at dancing school. I was very forward with those little girls and sometimes my conquests were marveled at by my various schoolfellows. But after we came to Memphis I found myself strangely timid with such girls. I was now able to pursue only the wildest sort of little girls that I met in the big public school I was put in. This change in myself worried me. But I was unable to discuss it with my new Memphis friend Alex Mercer or with my older brother Georgie (nothing like that ever worried Georgie) and certainly not with my father. Father and I might confer about many things but we never so much as acknowledged between us that sex existed.

When I said to Mother once during those years that I thought Father had ruined all our lives, except his own—by removing us to Memphis just when he did—she burst into laughter. And I immediately laughed with her. There was always something about her laughter that made anybody laugh with her. "How, my boy?" she asked. "Please tell me how at your tender age your life has been ruined?"

"I could tell you if I wanted to," I replied. "But it wouldn't be any use. You would only laugh at me. And it doesn't matter." Now she laughed even more gleefully. I was at that time winding up my last year in high school. I was a good scholar, like my father. I was excelling in all my classes, was editor of the school newspaper, was very near to being the star of the track team. I was a member of a social fraternity and was secretly having dates with girls whose very acquaintance I would have denied if questioned by my parents. And I had already begun to collect rare books and first editions. This last was something I would have hated Father knowing about almost as much as the existence of the wild little high school girls I knew. I confess that it would seem improbable, to say the least, that my life had already been ruined. Yet at the time I sincerely feared that it had, and I am not certain even now that it had not, though to attribute the responsibility to my father or to the move to Memphis would seem less a certainty. No doubt it was thinking of all that that made Mother laugh so when I said my life was ruined but that "it didn't matter."

"Ah, honey-lamb," she said to me presently, "don't become a cynic so early in life. I can't imagine what's driven you to this despair. Don't tell me *you* are wanting to get married, too! And that your father is standing in the way!"

"Oh, no," I said quickly and forcefully, revealing that I had given the matter considerable thought, "that's a mistake I'll never make. I'll never get married." Mother continued to go into little bursts of laughter for several moments. Then suddenly she frowned—making deep ridges in her forehead —and she puckered her lips, poutingly.

"Have we set you such a bad example of that sacred institution?" she asked presently. But she was only pretending to be hurt. Now she was laughing at me again and saying: "I can't imagine you want to miss out on life's most wonderful experience—that is, raising up a fine family!"

"Like ours, you mean?" I said. And of course now I was laughing with her again. But it was hard for me to think of this delightful and amusing person who only laughed at every serious thing I said as the same person who had treated me tenderly and sympathetically during all my childhood and who had been understanding of all my fears and managed to instill courage in me in moments when I was beginning to feel myself a coward. Even now it seems impossible she was the same woman. But even that day when she was laughing so cruelly at my adolescent experience and really refusing to hear how it was I felt my life was ruined, I remember suddenly having an image of her as she had been one day at

Nashville when I was eight or nine years old. . . . From our house on Franklin Pike I was going to ride my pony to school that day, as I nearly always did, and as it was the custom for most of the children at Robertson's Academy to do. But when I got as far as our front gate my pony, which was actually a hard-mouthed little horse named Red, and not a pony at all really, balked and refused to pass through the gateway. He reared and kicked when I switched his flanks and once even brought his head around as if to bite my knee. Mother must have been watching from an upstairs window of the house. In fact, she must have watched me having similar troubles with Red for several mornings before that. I suspect that for some time I had been showing signs of being afraid of the horse and perhaps of all horses and that Mother realized how disastrous this might be for me, considering the horsey world we then lived in, in those Nashville days. She quickly changed into riding clothes that morning, ran out to the stable, and with the aid of the stable boy saddled her horse and soon had ridden up beside me at the front gate. By the time she arrived, there were tears in my eyes, though I was not actually crying. "Let's get this critter on the road," she said as she trotted through the gateway on her little roan mare. Red moved right along beside her. The two horses were known to be friends and were often seen together, grazing in the pasture. "That Red is developing a nasty disposition," Mother said. "He's getting old, I suppose."

"He hates me especially, I think," I said.

Mother gave me a warm, encouraging smile. "They're stupid beasts," she said as we trotted on, side by side. "They're not like dogs. They hate us all. They only like themselves, just the way we stupid human beasts do." She and I smiled at each other with satisfaction. She rode beside me the two miles down the Pike, and when we reached the white gravel lane that led to Robertson's Academy she threw me a kiss, reined her horse around, and headed for home. I entered the lane and rode triumphantly up to the schoolhouse.

Five or six years later, in Memphis, it was sometimes hard to think of her as the same woman. I don't know still whether the trauma of the move changed her or whether the move from Nashville to Memphis merely happened to coincide with alterations in her mood and character. Or it may be that at some time, perhaps several years past, she had reached the limits of her sympathetic nature, maybe that she was by nature a good mother to children so long as they *were* children but not after they became adolescents and grown-up children.

3

WHEN MY MOTHER died two years ago, after nearly thirty years of real or imagined invalidism in Memphis, Father was already past eighty and my sisters were in their mid-fifties. Despite the sadness of it there was very naturally a certain relief felt by everyone that the old lady had got her release. Father suffered from various ailments associated with old age, but generally speaking he had everything under control. As I have said, it never occurred to me that he would have any such ordeal with his family as did those old men I remembered from my early days in Memphis. But it did occur to my old friend Alex Mercer, who also remembered those old widowers. Even at the funeral, when he and I were riding together in one of the undertaker's limousines—Alex is so close a friend, not just of mine but of all the family, that he and his wife were with the family throughout that day—he then tried to point out rather too subtly perhaps the danger that could lie ahead. He mentioned that Mr. George, as he always spoke of Father, might now become closer to certain of his friends than he had been before. I didn't understand that he meant women friends and thought he was merely taking refuge in platitudes, as Alex sometimes does on trying occasions. Within a few weeks of course Alex was writing me that I ought to feel proud of how well my sisters were behaving. He said it made him feel that human nature during the past thirty years (in Memphis, at least) had taken a step forward. He reported that Betsy and Josephine, who each had long since moved into a house of her own and in addition to establishing their real estate business, had, each of them, asserted her independence in every way imaginable (except for marriage), had now to their everlasting credit showed no signs of taking on a wifely or a protective role of any kind with their father. In fact they had, as I have already mentioned, almost immediately begun teasing him playfully about old ladies of his acquaintance. They had begun doing this almost too soon, Alex Mercer presumed to point out. But when Alex wrote me, as he did almost every week during this period, he tried to put the best face on it. "At least," he wrote, "this indelicacy on their parts is better than *the other thing*." By which he meant, of course, better than the kind of fate that had befallen those other old men both he and I remembered.

Alex is a professor of English at Memphis State University, and it is interesting to see him employing his imagination in an almost literary way on everything and everybody he wishes to understand. He could not be a more different sort of person than he is from my two sisters, and yet in his letters I could see him trying to enter into their experience with all possible sympathy. One could so easily imagine, he wrote me about this matter—in his rather stilted prose style, one could so easily imagine one or the other of my two sisters telephoning their father one day to invite him to her house for dinner (either sister it might be) and could so easily imagine her learning from the houseman or the cook ("over the telephone, mind you, which would only add of course to the danger of offense"), learning, that is, that the father, the widowed Mr. George, was already engaged for dinner that particular evening—at Mrs. Eva Caldwalder's house, say, or at Mrs. Caroline Merriwether's. One could imagine the unreasonable, personal jealousy this might incite on the part of any such unmarried, middle-aged daughter of Memphis, and could imagine the just resentment to be felt by such a daughter for the sake of her so recently deceased mother. In that event, if feeling should run sufficiently high against any particular widow-lady (so Alex wrote me)—be it Mrs. Caldwalder or Mrs. Merriwether, or any other—then certainly there might be something that I, as son to Mr. George, ought to worry about. Because, as Alex went on to point out, there was no knowing what stratagem two unmarried, middle-aged sisters such as Betsy and Josephine Carver might resort to in order to restrict or restrain the romantic adventures of their father.

I believe I can state categorically that not just my friend Alex Mercer but everybody else in Memphis who lived in the east end of town and knew women like my sisters was aware of what Betsy's and Josephine's feelings would likely be so soon after their old mother had died. Something worse than what happened to Colonel Fielding or Judge Gaston or Mr. Manning might happen.

But happily of course it did not turn out so—not at least in relation to those old ladies. My two sisters exhibited no resentment whatsoever concerning their father's new role. Within a month—within weeks really after their mother's death—a variety of "amusing stories" began to circulate, stories that clearly came from Betsy and Jo themselves. Humorous, good-natured stories they were, indulgent, even endearing accounts of how Mr. George was being "courted" by eighty-and ninety-year-old ladies, the grandes dames of Memphis, so to speak. Some of these ladies even dispatched uniformed black chauffeurs to fetch the old widower to their houses and if the weather during dinner hour took a turn for the worse or if the evening simply ran on too late the hostess would invite the attractive Mr. George Carver to occupy her lavender-scented guest room for the night.

There were funny little incidents and episodes reported too, of laughter on porches after midnight and of screeches even, down in the garden, accounts of Mr. George putting his hat on sidewise before a looking glass in a front hallway when he was leaving—a little tipsy perhaps, he *and* the ladies —and all the ladies calling him "Mr. Bonaparte," because of his hat. Nobody quite knew what those stories implied, because nobody ever quite knows what such old people really do when the evening grows late. It is something people often find embarrassing even to contemplate. But my sisters Betsy and Josephine Carver clearly delighted in these accounts of their father's high spirits with the old ladies. Such stories *couldn't* be anything but innocent, they insisted. The stories made Father seem laughable and ridiculous, but my sisters did not mind that. After all, Alex more than once assured me, my two sisters didn't want Mr. George pining away for "Miss Minta," which was how Alex always spoke of my mother.

By this time in life my two sisters were well known in Memphis for possessing, each of them, a felicitous if sometimes cruel sense of humor. They were known for inventing wickedly funny anecdotes about their own friends and contemporaries. It is a kind of humor we have all been familiar with on the part of Southern ladies of a certain age. And now the sudden flood of such stories from Betsy and Jo might have seemed predictable and quite acceptable if Mr. George had been anyone other than their own doted-upon father and if they had not been famous locally as two such daddy's girls as they actually were. Wasn't it, otherwise, just the kind of humor they were always indulging in? Certainly all who knew my sisters well were accustomed for many years now to hearing this kind of mockery from them.

And yet to Alex Mercer's ears this mockery of their father, who had always been such a special favorite of his own, seemed as unbecoming as it was unpredictable. Their general levity on the subject of Father's evenings with those old ladies had a quality Alex wasn't prepared for, actually had a certain suggestiveness about it that left him feeling uneasy about how the situation might inevitably involve me, their brother. I was not only Alex's closest friend but someone whose mode of life, off in Manhattan, worried him at times and at other times gave him, I think, vicarious satisfaction. There is a certain serenity about the free and independent sort of life I live here that a Memphis family man cannot fail to envy, living as I do, that is, with a woman some fifteen years younger than myself and having for my friends intellectual people who have no more involvement with the dull, practical problems of domestic life than I do. Alex felt I would be profoundly shaken if events there at home went the way he thought surely they would go, would be shaken, that is, if he did not prepare me for what he considered the likely inevitability. My sisters of course put some of their stories about Father in their letters to me. But probably one did not get the full effect in those letters that Alex Mercer got when hearing the two sisters actually tell those stories to a roomful of people. For it was their manner and tone that Alex found offensive.

In my reply to Alex's letters of warning, I said that Betsy's and Josephine's offense lay *only* in their manner and tone and that perhaps this was merely my sisters' way of making the story amusing. I said I supposed it came to them very naturally since they had always told just such stories about their friends in this ladylike way that was at the same time suggestive. I knew the suggestiveness may have been only in how they rolled their eyes or raised their plucked eyebrows. (Though they were showing signs of age by this time, Betsy and Josephine still plucked their eyebrows and shaved their legs, just as they had done when they were nineteen.) I knew well enough the kind of thing Alex was reporting to me. Alex and I together had in former days often been with my two sisters at the kind of big Memphis Christmas parties which people of all ages attend, and we had there seen them surrounded sometimes by a devoted little band of contemporaries whom they were electrifying with one of their innocent-seeming anecdotes. One didn't ever forget such a scene. At some point Betsy's ladylike voice would quaver— or perhaps it would be Josephine's (their very voices had now become so very much alike)—the voice would quaver and tremble seemingly on purpose, as if to insist upon the lady's delicacy of feeling. It was a quality one felt one had heard in recitations of Southern ladies of my mother's generation. But presently there would come a roar of laughter from the encircling little band of friends, a roar which ladies of Mother's generation (in Nashville, at any rate) would not have been capable of, and one knew that with a single phrase or with a roll of the eyes or the artful lifting of a plucked eyebrow Betsy or Josephine had turned her own innocent story into a veritable shocker.

It was all very good-natured of course. But their stories about their father even without a roll of the eyes or the lift of an eyebrow seemed almost *too* amusing and *too* good-natured. It seemed too good-natured to be believed in, somehow. It made Alex and some other listeners in the circle increasingly uneasy—uneasy for Father's well-being, that is. But on the other hand, despite Alex's letters, I, Phillip Carver —off in my New York apartment—would have none of that! We should all welcome the benign spirit of my two sisters, I wrote Alex. Surely their merriment in the matter must come

to everyone as a welcome change. Surely it wasn't what anyone on the scene could have expected. To think, I wrote, that
there could be this instance down there in Memphis of middle-
aged children—and two doting, unmarried daughters at that
—behaving so leniently and generously toward a widowed
old father and especially toward a father known to possess a
not inconsiderable fortune. It was clear at least, wasn't it, that
these two daughters of his did not intend sending Mr. George
Carver off to some plantation "manor house" in the Mississippi Delta or to a well-guarded "private hospital" in East
Memphis.

If there were moments when I doubted my sisters' actual
sincerity in the present circumstances, I think it was mostly
because it was just too hard for *any*one to believe that there
were two such Memphis women as these, present there, that
is to say, before all the world, accepting changes and developments in their old father's life which similar women in an
earlier generation would almost certainly have been mightily
disturbed by. To Alex Mercer during this period it seemed
almost that the millennium had come. Could it be, he put it
to me in his rhetorical, academic way, that during the past
two decades when the world was learning to recognize the
rights of young people and the rights of women and the rights
of the colored races it had also learned to respect the rights
of old people—the right at least of an old widower to live
out his life as he chose? What seemed most glorious and
most inconceivable to me, off in New York, was not that this
could have happened in the great world at large but could
have happened even down there in the small, old world of
Memphis.

I HAVE TO SAY that despite all the natural affection
which I felt for my two sisters and despite all my gratitude

for their assistance in my finally getting away from Memphis when I was still not yet thirty and despite gratitude also for their having tried to assist me still earlier when I wished to marry a girl I was in love with in Chattanooga (and there has never been another), still, every time I went home, particularly in recent years, I dreaded the sight of them—the first sight of them, that is—and dreaded still more my first conversation with them after my arrival.

I have already made reference to the independent lives they had come to live. Their peculiar kind of independence was, as a matter of fact, the thing in their lives they had seemed for many years now to value most in the world. And with Father they somehow felt the necessity to assert this independence more vigorously every year that passed. Though they had yielded to him in not marrying the young men they had loved when they were young ladies they seemed to feel justified in yielding to his wishes in nothing else afterward. At the time of the removal to Memphis both girls were made to feel that their conformity, their obedience, their moral support was the then most important matter in their father's life. And they did conform, they obeyed, they supported— they did not marry. But when at last the family crisis had passed, they became known as the two most independent young women in Memphis and were frequently referred to, according to Alex Mercer, as "those two awful Nashville girls" and finally as "the wildest things that ever got inside the Memphis Junior League."

Though it is my firm opinion that neither sister has ever to this day slept with a man (and I believe I have good evidence to the effect), from an early time after we had moved to Memphis they seemed determined to give the impression, both in conversation and in all appearances, of its being an almost nightly ritual with them. My very earliest recollection of them was of course back in Nashville when they seemed gentle, ladylike, submissive Southern girls. That is how everyone in Nashville must surely remember them. But in Memphis almost from the beginning they were known as two young ladies who lived with the same independence that usually only young gentlemen there enjoyed. They very early, and over Father's protest, entered the real estate business. They took up golf and tennis and swimming, and found no trouble in defeating men who dared compete with them in those sports. They never became masculine in appearance or in their manner or behavior generally, but they let it be known certainly that they were in competition with every man who came their way. Soon they had founded their very own real estate firm, instead of continuing to be employed by male "realtors." (The term had just come into use then and was ridiculed by Father as a "Memphis vulgarism.") And soon afterward, without so much as a by-your-leave to Father, they bought residences of their own only a few blocks from where our parents then lived and set up their own separate domestic establishments.

It was from those establishments, comfortable, two-story houses with canvas awnings reaching out over all windows and extending from the porches, too, that they were so useful to my brother George and me whenever we wished to achieve some degree of independence for ourselves. George was in Father's law firm for a while but since he was unhappy there he pretended he had been drafted into the Army, though actually he volunteered, and went off to war. My sisters helped him deceive Father in the matter and made it possible for him to go off to Europe and get himself killed, which I assume had become his own chief purpose in life.

But if Betsy and Josephine stood ready always to assist Georgie and me in our assertion of any kind of independence, they never failed in their affectionate attention to Father. Their love and admiration for the man seemed boundless. I suppose they otherwise could never have submitted to his wishes with regard to Wyant Brawley and Clarkson Manning. They had words of praise for Father in every sphere of his life. They would tell you he had the best taste in clothes of any man in Memphis, always praising his attire, everything from his shoestrings to his ties. They would tell you that he had the best judgment about politics of anyone, the keenest business sense, and of course the profoundest knowledge of the law. Alex Mercer used often to write me about seeing them and Father together. Alex lauded my sisters for being so attentive to the old man. Alex had, of course, always been a tremendous admirer of my father and was ever critical of me for going off to New York after the War and leaving Father with no son to depend upon. Alex used to urge me in letters to get myself an academic degree of an advanced kind and come back and teach, as he did, at one of the city's institutions of higher learning. It was an outlandish idea of course, but it did sometimes make me think of how it would have been to have remained at home, like Alex Mercer, with some easy academic job or other and, like Alex—with his wife, Frances, and his five or six children (I can never remember just how many it is he has)—living over near Southwestern College or out near Memphis State University in one of those tile-roofed Memphis bungalows on the periphery of, but not part of, the Memphis world that Alex and I had known when we were young. It is a neighborhood that is farther away, in a sense, from the life lived by Father and my two sisters than is my life with Holly in our 82nd Street apartment, in Manhattan. At any rate, in his letters Alex would tell me that you could rarely go to Father's law office without seeing one of my sisters there, either beside him at his desk consulting him about some real estate contract or merely lounging about in his front reception room, sometimes sitting there—whichever of them it was—with her head resting on a chair back and her eyes closed and perhaps with her crossed ankles stretched out before her on the deep pile of the carpet and sometimes even with a cigarette dangling from her lips. Or Alex would tell me about seeing both sisters at lunch with Father on Saturday at the Tennessee Club or at one of the downtown restaurants or at supper on Sunday night at the Country Club. Alex would even say explicitly that he thought my sisters were trying to make it up to Father for his not having a son to whom he could turn. Yet I am confident that Alex was wrong in this last supposition. Whatever my sisters' motive was, it was not that.

Long before this it was perfectly clear to me of course that neither Betsy nor Josephine was ever going to marry. Yet their incredibly girlish talk, at age fifty and more, about the possibility of marriage for them continued right up until the time I am speaking of. One would have had to call it mere banter, I suppose. Whenever I came home for a brief visit (all my visits were as brief as I could decently make them) each sister would tell me whom the other was "dating." And this was true when both women were past fifty and were fully in command of their large and successful real estate business. Sometimes their confidences would be couched differently. I would be told by one of them who it was the other was "having an affair with." It was almost as if, like two children, they didn't know the meaning of the words and phrases they used. (It was such impressions as this that supported my conviction that in reality they were still virgins.) Or often as not, on other occasions, I would be met at the plane when I arrived by one of them in the company of some good-looking, well-dressed man of fifty or so—frequently a rather effeminate-seeming man. Later when he was no longer with us and we were alone in the car or when we were at our parents' house, where I would be staying, I would be asked my opinion of the man I had just met. "What manner of man do you take him for, Phil?" I might be asked. Or more directly: "What would you think of *him* as a brother-in-law?" Sometimes I would indulge them and go along with the question as though it made sense, as though there were a real possibility of marriage for them. Sometimes I would even give my unfavorable impression of the man I had just met. My sister was apt to laugh coyly and say something teasing like: "You're just a jealous brother. He's *so* good-looking!" But if I was tired from the flight I had just arrived on, I might only smile and say that I knew that she—whichever sister it was—wasn't actually thinking of marrying the fellow. And the reply then would be something like: "We may surprise you yet, Phil dear." But as for me, I felt certain they never would. And of course, as it turned out, they never did.

Such talk about their beaux was not always done in private—not by any means. The talk with me was a mere echo of or perhaps sometimes a foreshadowing of the talking they did in Father's presence and for his special benefit. When the family was gathered at the table in the dining room one of my middle-aged sisters would begin teasing the other about some suitor, so called. It was done in the best of spirits and was also received so. Mother, nearing eighty by this time and delighting if she were attentive at all in these family games, would declare that she had reached the point at which she would settle for any semblance of a son-in-law, by which she intended to be making a joke—a very broad joke for *her*. She meant to imply, all in fun of course (it was a part of this game they played), that she had not only given up discriminating between sorts of men her daughters might marry but was prepared even, if her daughters preferred it, to accept some unconventional arrangement like my own with Holly Kaplan. Father would pretend to be shocked by Mother's so incautiously urging her unmarried, aging daughters into something worse or less than marriage. He would pretend to enjoy the game, but it was easy to see he was made uncomfortable by it. Yet in the spirit of fun he would proceed to speak most judiciously about the old bachelor or widower or divorcé in question and to assert that he was sure the man's intentions were honorable. He knew as well as Mother, of course, and as well as I that there was no real possibility of marriage or of any alliance of any kind for Betsy or Josephine.

When these conversations—or travesties upon conversations—took place I would be at home on one of my seasonal visits. I think it was this silly twaddle between my aging sisters and my aged parents that made me most dread my visits home. It was as if the whole family had finally become completely demented and didn't know how consummately and irreversibly life had already passed us by. Or sometimes it seemed to me that it was I who was out of my head or that I was simply dreaming all of this, confusing the past and the present, as one generally does in dreams. But after a few days at home I would get used to it. I would still wonder to myself, though, how they could indulge in this play year after year.

DURING THE FIRST years that I lived in New York I used to feel guilty sometimes about the kind of constraint Betsy and Josephine were under compared to the life I lived. I used to mention this feeling to them when I went home, but they would only laugh at me and say that I did not know how free they were. I knew the truth of the matter, though. I recognized their charade for what it was. I knew the restraint they had put *themselves* under for life. And I would tell them that I thought I might yet change my career and come home to live, in order to share with them some of the responsibilities of having very old parents. I told them I knew how often in the night they were called upon to get up and drive the length of the city when Mother was having one of her nervous episodes or Father an attack of neuropathy. But they dismissed the idea with a shake of the head and a wave of the hand. They wouldn't hear to my giving up my career in New York. That was where I belonged. That was where I had to be to do my work. After all, I was a man, they said, as though they were not doing a man's work in their real estate and insurance business. And after all, it was they, my big sisters, who had sent me out into the world, wasn't it? It was they who had seen to it that I got away from that home environment of ours. It was from Betsy's house and with money borrowed from Josephine that I had set out for New York. That had been one of the great satisfactions in their life, so they said, and I would look at them then and seeing how they had aged I would remind myself again of all my indebtedness to them for having the serene, reasonable life I now had.

In another, earlier time, of course, Betsy and Josephine would have been called spinsters. And no doubt they would then have lived in the house with their old people and would have dressed and behaved considerably older than the married women their own age—that is, as a mark of the special respect due two virginal ladies. As a matter of fact, they did dress and behave differently from the married women who were their contemporaries. But not in the way it would have been in another era. The difference in their attire when they had got to be fifty was toward the opposite end of the pole. From their mid-forties forward, as a matter of fact, they dressed more like young girls than like their married contemporaries, some of whom were already grandmothers, of course, with half-grown grandchildren.

In those days my sisters were still women of enormous energy. In addition to managing their business firm they led an almost frenzied social life. Of this I had accounts all through the years from Alex. But also Betsy and Josephine were forever boasting to me when I was at home not just of the ladies' luncheons they attended and the downtown business brunches but of the debutante and Cotton Carnival parties—the balls for their friends' daughters and granddaughters —which they still, themselves, attended, as well as of their late-night visits to those certain night spots which they frequented with their men friends. According to Alex, their innumerable social activities were counted amongst the seven wonders of the Memphis social scene. He pointed out that with the passing of years they had progressed from being regarded as "those awful Nashville girls" to being, themselves, fully accepted as a remarkable Memphis institution. But above all, or despite all, according to Alex Mercer's letters to me, they had in one respect at least become the laughingstock of the town. And this was what often embarrassed me at the airport when I arrived or when I was departing. The awful fact was that with figures by no means any longer youthful they often got themselves up in the most extreme fashions that only the most sylphlike and dashing young girls should have worn in any given year—even the most daring fashions, one might say. If, for instance, low backs were favored for evening gowns, their backs would be bare down to the divide in their rather sizable buttocks. Or if particularly low necklines were in vogue, then theirs would plunge between mountainous breasts practically to the navel. If slit skirts were the fashion, then my sisters' would be vented well above the knees, exposing fleshy thighs which by this time in my sisters' lives were indeed of no inconsiderable size. Whenever I was at home I had ample opportunity to observe that all Alex told me about them was true. They would sometimes come by Father's house before they went out of an evening to ask Father and me to inspect their ridiculous getups. If we were shocked, then they would laugh uproariously. Sometimes I felt their appearance was as big a joke to themselves as to everyone else. But laughingstock or not, I could seldom manage a smile even at the grotesquery of my sisters' costumes or at the awful incongruity of their figures with the alluring postures they assumed. Because I would always see in them still vestiges of the beautiful older sisters of my Nashville boyhood.

Always it was one of them who met me at the airport when I arrived or who was there to see me off at my departure. Often as not this was during the daylight hours, and in that case I took no notice of their clothes, because their businesslike daytime clothing did not reflect their concern for youthful fashions. But if it was near the cocktail hour or perhaps later in the evening when my plane came down or lifted off, there one of them was sure to be—or sometimes both of them—so spectacularly decked out in high heels and perfect coiffure (Josephine kept her hair black as ever, and Betsy saw to it that hers was the same honey-blonde color it had been when she was a girl), both of them so richly got up in their party clothes and jewelry and dyed hair that I would find myself standing first on one foot and then the other as, surrounded by a crowd of Memphis onlookers, we waited for the baggage to appear or waited in a similar crowd for the time when the gates would open and I could at last board the plane for La Guardia.

After every such send-off in Memphis it was wonderfully comforting and reassuring to see Holly Kaplan when I had come in from La Guardia to 82nd Street. Her sensible, brown, bobbed hair with a little white beginning to appear, especially in the straight bangs on her forehead, and her flat-heeled shoes and the short-sleeved white blouse above the dark skirt and the simple wristwatch her only jewelry, it all said to me about Memphis just what Manhattan had seemed to say to me about Memphis on the first day I had arrived there: Life doesn't *have* to be like that life in Memphis.

4

On one occasion when I came in from La Guardia, Holly met me in the front loggia of our apartment. She didn't usually make such an effort to welcome me, but it was rather late in the evening and I suppose when she heard me fumbling with my keys in the three locks we have on our door she felt she had to make certain it was I who was trying to enter and not some intruder. (We live in one of the safer neighborhoods on the Upper West Side, but still we have to be very careful.) When finally I got the door open I was so glad to see her I dropped my bag and threw my arms about her. I at once felt her body stiffen from her astonishment at this demonstration. Presently she said to me accusingly: "It must have been worse than usual this time."

"Much worse," said I, though actually it had not been so. It was simply that on this occasion both sisters had come out in their finery to put me on the plane. When I released Holly from my embrace, she took up my bag and carried it back to the bedroom for me. (Holly is such a feminist that she doesn't miss an opportunity like that.) I went directly to the kitchen and began putting together a midnight supper for myself. After a few minutes she came in and sat down opposite me at the little enameled table where I was eating. She was smoking a cigarette, I remember—something she didn't often do so late in the evening unless she was working on some bad page proof or was otherwise annoyed about something. I began to regale her with accounts of my sisters' doings and of their efforts sometimes to vex and sometimes to please Father. Suddenly, with a sigh, Holly blew out a great billow of smoke and said irritably that I *was really* absolutely obsessed with my family!

This was an accusation which Holly and I frequently hurled at each other. In the beginning our complaints about our families had been perhaps our deepest bond. We had long since, however, worn out the subject. And so I said not another word about my visit home on that occasion. And when several months later letters began coming about Father's "stepping out," I had to keep all that bottled up within me.

But on the Sunday night when Betsy and Jo called me about Father's marriage plans with Mrs. Clara Stockwell I thought again about Holly's response to the subject of my family that earlier time as well as on a good many other similar occasions. Because, you see, during the course of that evening after I made my decision and when I was making my flight reservations and packing my bag I thought of telephoning Holly to say I was going to Memphis. But I knew that any reference to my concern about Father and what he might suffer at the hands of my sisters would be the cause of both amusement and annoyance to her. I would finally leave the apartment next morning without communicating with her in any way. At the time this seemed to me to mean that the break between us was really permanent.

I was wakeful all night that night. But it was not Holly who was on my mind. It was my father. In my mind I kept going over the letters I had received from Betsy and Jo with their good-natured reports of his evenings with the old ladies and their later letters with indulgent accounts of his "stepping out" with women of a different sort. But I thought also of the letters I had had from Alex Mercer on the same subjects. It seemed strange that my sisters would have written in such detail about Father's evenings in the different midtown night spots or that they *could* actually have done so without themselves having been present. For it did not actually occur to me when the letters came that they might have been so. To anyone but me it might have seemed still stranger that Alex Mercer could have been motivated to pass on to me his rather less than responsible son Howard's accounts of having seen my father in those places. To understand his going on at such length about Father one had to remember Alex Mercer as a boy and remember the deep admiration he had felt for my father from the first moment he set eyes on him.

WHAT A GREAT comfort it was to me, during the first days after my father moved us to Memphis, to have made friends with such a boy as Alex Mercer. I had come from Nashville after the fall term of school had already begun. But within a few days I was entered in the eighth grade at Bruce School. My father went with me to the principal's office on a Monday morning and saw that I was properly registered. It turned out that the principal was an old gentleman who had once been headmaster of the Thornton Academy, and Father had known him there. It was the sort of thing that was always happening to us during the first year in Memphis. The rest of the family was always having to wait while Father enjoyed a reunion with some old-timer from Thornton. All our trade had to be taken to a grocery store or a dry cleaner or a service station operated by some character out of Father's past in Thorn County. On the day of my registration at Bruce School I had to endure a half hour of reunion in the principal's office. Finally I was slipped unobtrusively into an English class that was already in session. In that very first class on that very first day I was given a desk to share with Alex. I won't ever forget the look he fixed me with when I slid into the seat beside him. It was both cordial and cold—warmly cordial and coldly observant. As he would tell me many times afterward I was that day the most exotic human animal he had ever set eyes upon, and he would not at that moment have believed it possible that when he would see my father for the first time a few weeks later he would find that tall man from Nashville, wearing striped trousers at noon, an even stranger, more exotic-looking creature.

I was, myself, dressed that first day in knee britches and wearing a sort of Buster Brown, highly starched collar. Though I considered myself already a lady's man and had been so very forward with those little girls at the Nashville dancing school and at the horse show, still I was dressed as boys would have been dressed in the eighth grade of Mr. Wallace's private school in Nashville. But Memphis was a public school town at that time and boys my age there wore long trousers and soft-collared shirts.

It seemed to Alex Mercer that I had dropped from another planet. Not only were my clothes different from Memphis boys', my hair was cut differently—we wore it longer at Mr. Wallace's—and my speech was most decidedly different. (Even to the present day my sisters and I are said to have more of a Nashville than a Memphis accent.) I said "gull" for girl and "bud" for bird. Soon Alex would notice that I carried my books like a girl, in the crook of my arm. And I walked more like a little boy than an adolescent. Moreover, I had about me still some of the pudginess of infancy. (I had been quite fat as a small boy.) It was this, I think, that accounted for Alex's first question to me when English class was over on that first day when I slipped into the seat beside him. "How old are you, Phil?" he asked. I confessed I had just turned thirteen. But there was nothing ugly in the tone of his question and nothing in his face afterward to make me feel uncomfortable. Because Alex Mercer was ever the most tactful and sympathetic male of the species that one could possibly imagine.

But Alex could certainly not at the time have imagined that I, in my Buster Brown collar and knickers, could already have had the kind of "young adult" experience I had had before leaving Nashville. It is difficult for me now to imagine myself in such clothes when saying goodbye to the grown-up-looking little girl in the Dutch bob. On the actual occasion of our parting, that little girl's and mine, we had met as often before by the old brick tower on the campus of Ward Belmont, the girls' school she attended. And as at most earlier meetings she had for me a rather handsome present, wrapped in tissue paper and tied with white ribbons. No matter how grown-up our relationship was, there were some things about it, like the frequent presents, that I did not understand at the time. But it did not seem strange to me that Evelyn was six inches taller than I, that she wore a dress not unlike those I saw my older sisters wearing, that there were moderately high heels on her white pumps. Her dark hair was cut in a bob that might have been worn by any young lady or any little girl in those days.

We kissed when we met that day, as we had long since grown accustomed to doing. We were both very much aware of its being our last meeting, and our kiss and embrace was held for a longer time than was usual with us—that is, for a weekday afternoon on the school grounds. "You won't write from Memphis," she said at once. "Boys never write. Still I'm giving you this, just as a little hint." I opened the small, elongated package, somewhat embarrassed at my never having given her a present, and expressed my genuine admiration for the gold-banded fountain pen. We talked there for a while, and when finally I began saying goodbye, aware of the tears in my own eyes and even aware of the emptiness I knew I would feel for a long time afterward, I could find no words to tell her how disturbed I was by our parting. Then I noticed suddenly how her eyes had rolled back into her head. She had literally fainted away, and I stood there by the brick tower holding her in my arms and with tears now streaming down my cheeks. The confusion I felt, however, is what mainly I recall about the moment. And it remains confusing to me now when I think of the thirteen-year-old boy in his little-boy clothes holding the girl that was in all appearances and perhaps in all feelings a grown-up young woman. I try to think sometimes, moreover, of what confused feelings she must have experienced about her lover coming to her dressed as I was in my starched collar and my brown knickers, buttoned at the knee.

WITHIN A WEEK or so Alex Mercer had me wearing long trousers and a proper shirt. My hair was cut shorter. I carried my books in the approved manner—that is, alongside my hip or thigh, with my arm hanging straight down from shoulder to wrist. Had I not had Alex's advice and protection, the transition and settling in at Memphis would have been much more difficult for me. Perhaps the old principal or the pretty English teacher knew what a good move it would be to put me under his care. Although he was almost feminine in his awareness and in his concern for the feelings and the experience of other people, Alex was otherwise the epitome of masculinity in a boy just entering adolescence. He was a kind of norm for twelve- and thirteen-year-old Memphis boys.

He was so much so that he was always looked to whenever there was an election of leaders on the playground or in the homeroom. It was, in fact, this very quality in himself that Alex loathed at that age and at every later age as well. This being the perfect norm, he felt, was characteristic not just of himself but of his entire family. "We're nothing but plain Memphis—pure Memphis from the word go," he used to say to me. "Nothing more. Nothing less." His brothers and sisters, unlike my own, were well-adjusted people, always being held up as ideals by their schoolmates. But as Alex liked to remark later in his life, they never amounted to a great deal after school years. And both of his parents were also Memphis to the core. Their forebears had lived there, as the local saying was, since before the Yellow Fever. Both Mercer parents, according to Alex, were convinced that any deviation from what they considered the Memphis norm, any eccentricity or any excellence of any kind amounted only to exhibitionism. The best human being, said Alex's father, was the human being best adjusted to the circumstances he was born into. Alex's was a family, said this son of Memphis who was to take such an interest in my own family, that saw the whole world from the point of view of that spot in midtown Memphis where Madison Avenue crossed Cleveland Street. They believed, so Alex said, that you could see all you needed to see of the world from a ride on the crosstown streetcar. But about Alex Mercer himself there was something that made him forever fascinated by and sympathetic to that which he perhaps yearned after in spirit but which practically speaking he did not wish himself to become. His was by no means the simplest way of looking at the world, but it made him the best kind of friend I could have happened upon in my new life.

My father appeared on the Bruce School playground one day to fetch me home, because my mother was sick and was asking for me. That was when Alex saw Father for the first time. It was, so to speak, love at first sight for both of them. It wasn't an easy moment for Alex. Here he had no more than got me straightened out with regard to long trousers and a correct haircut than there appeared before him a towering human creature even more foreign than I had seemed, in his attire and in general appearance. With Father's panache of coal-black hair, his tall, straight figure, and his athletic physique, he still looked almost heroically youthful. It was partly the contrast of his natural, youthful appearance with his formal, old-fashioned way of dressing that made the stunning impression which he produced on nearly everyone he met in Memphis. Unlike other Memphis businessmen he frequently went to his office wearing striped trousers and a cutaway jacket—a morning suit, no less—along with a starched wing collar and a gray four-in-hand silk tie. That is how he was got up when he came for me on the playground. And for Alex he was like some romantic figure out of a past age stepping into his own everyday, commonsense Memphis world.

I think Father was ever afterward for Alex like a body of belief that he could not quite give his personal credence to but whose truth he devoutly respected and held to be a philosophical absolute. My own view of Father was not nearly so high-flown or complicated. For me he was flesh and blood and until the day I left Memphis behind, to take up residence in Manhattan, he remained simply a barrier between me and any independent life I might aspire to—a barrier to any pursuit of ideas, interests, goals that my temperament guided me toward. As early as that day on the playground I had actually already been in Memphis just long enough to see this man as something strange and phenomenal, even as something of a clownish figure.

Yet from that day forward—and without Alex's alienating me as a friend—Alex Mercer and my father, Mr. George Carver, seemed like kindred spirits, though in reality of course they were opposites attracting each other. It was a wonderful phenomenon to behold, and I have never anywhere seen notice taken of the kind of communication and imaginative interplay that can exist between a child and an adult acquainted with each other only as friends—not as child and parent or in any other kind of kinship. What it amounts to is the same sort of fulfillment that friends of any age are able to offer each other. And I must interject here that the relationship between Mr. Lewis Shackleford and my father may not originally have been very different from that between Alex and Father, because that other, old Nashville friendship began long before any business association between them, when Lewis Shackleford, seven or eight years younger than Father, was a little water boy on the football sidelines, indulging in hero worship and only waiting for the game to be over so that he could speak to his hero. It may be that my father was the natural embodiment of the ideal of big boy for many a little boy and that I simply happened to be of such a temperament and to possess such a cast of mind that he could not be my own ideal.

At any rate, that day on the playground when I mentioned Alex Mercer's name, Father stretched forth his hand to give

a manly handshake to the eager childlike adolescent hand
offered him. They smiled at each other rather timidly but
entered at once into easy conversation. Cordial relations between them never flagged during all the years afterward.
When Alex mentioned to his parents that night how formally
Father had been dressed, his mother said to his father: "Isn't
that typical Nashville pretension?" But *my* father said to me
that night at dinner that Alex was the best kind of Memphis
boy one was apt to find and a good companion for me to
have. Father said: "He's so forthright and warm and unpretentious." Neither Alex nor my father could have put it into
words at the time, and certainly I could not have done so then,
but I can say with authority now that what was established
between them that day was that Father would always represent for Alex a sophisticated, perhaps even a superficial, world
beyond the river town of Memphis, a world which he could
never hope to attain to, and that Alex would represent for
Father the real, reasonable, down-to-earth world of Memphis
that he would have to make his way into and become a part
of whether he liked doing so or not.

Through the years their mutual interest in and their
genuine admiration for each other not only continued but increased. Alex would come to our house and sit endlessly listening to Father while Father described episodes of his early life
that he never bothered to tell his own children about—or at
least not his sons. Georgie and I were free to listen to these
lengthy disquisitions, but Georgie, who was a full-fledged
teenager by then, would wander away. Georgie never took
an interest in the adult life around him—least of all perhaps in
Father's life—or in the history of our parents and their families. I would sometimes sit and listen when Father talked to
Alex, but Georgie would wander off into some other part of
the house, as if determined to get beyond the sound of

Father's voice. He did so in much the same spirit that he would eventually pull away from the family and go and get himself killed in the War. It was as if without understanding his own reasons he wished always to detach and disassociate himself from his own family and its history. It used to seem to me that it was simply a strong instinct he had—either for self-preservation or for self-destruction. Perhaps the rest of us had it too but with sufficient elements of reason and feeling mixed in to prevent our taking individual and separate action of a kind that would finally matter. For Georgie it was different. Within weeks after our coming to Memphis to live Georgie had cast off all traces of a Nashville accent in his speech and spoke during the rest of his short and unhappy life almost in the accents of a native-born Memphian. It was this quality of his, this adapting so readily as he did to Memphis and its general province, that tended to set him apart from the rest of the family and to some extent estranged him always from Betsy and Josephine and me and even from our parents, I think. Georgie was killed during the first hours of the invasion of the French coast. There was another Army pilot from Memphis who made his acquaintance just a few days before he met his death. That other Memphis pilot wrote to Mother afterward, saying that when he first heard Georgie's voice in a room next to the one where he was bunking, a few nights before the invasion, he knew at once that Georgie was someone from Memphis. "I knew at once from his voice," the young man wrote Mother, "not only that he was from Memphis but that he was from somewhere between Cooper and Crosstown and in the Anandale section of town." (Which was where my father bought a house only a year or so after we came to Memphis and where my sisters themselves would eventually buy their own houses.) "I could almost have placed him squarely on the corner of Belvedere and Harbert,

and that's where George told me next day he had grown up."
I think this letter identifying Georgie so indelibly as *of* and
from Memphis hurt us all nearly as much as the first news of
his death and was in a sense our final estrangement from him.
That's how it was for Georgie. It was not so for me, of course.
It was very different for me and Betsy and Jo. After we
moved to Memphis we went on saying "gull" for girl and
"bud" for bird, in the old Nashville way. I remember that Alex
Mercer took notice of my peculiar pronunciations and made
his mild fun of them. He managed to effect a good many
changes in my way of doing things but not in my speech. My
speech, as well as that of my sisters, continued to reflect what
we heard spoken at home more than what we heard spoken
among our Memphis peers.

Though I would sometimes sit and listen when Father
talked to Alex and while Georgie wandered off to another
part of the house, I did not really listen in any ordinary sense.
I was already familiar with most of the material, as I suppose
Georgie was too. What interested me was Father's tone when
speaking to Alex. It was precisely that which he would have
used with adults, as though Alex were one of his contemporaries, one of his own peers. I suppose one can't talk to one's
own children that way. (Though of course this can be merely
conjecture on my part since I have no children of my own.)
I think one must imagine that one's own children are too
much a part of one's self. A father—I do now conjecture—
finds it too utterly vexing when his children don't easily understand. But I believe it is a sign of remarkable intelligence
in a man—or in a woman—when like my father he does not
make categorical distinctions in his mind between other people, with regard to age or sex or race, but instead merely senses
the intelligence of every individual. Whatever may be said of
my father by me or by my sisters, he was not in the most

important sense, a respecter of persons. Although I may have seen him at certain rare times seem to undergo a total personality change in the presence of some great person who turned up in our midst—an extraordinarily rich man, a powerful judge, a famous politician—on most occasions he spoke to all people in the same soft, friendly, somewhat judicious tone. And this whether it was a servant or a civic leader or an old lady or a small child. It was this tone and manner of his that must always have first appealed to everyone who knew him, including my mother of course and including Mr. Lewis Shackleford. And it was with that warm, open, unprejudiced manner of his that he spoke to Alex that first day on the playground. It was so he would ever afterward speak to him.

I don't recall at what early period there began to be confidences between the two of them, but I do recall that when Alex was making his decision about whether to go into business with his father or to enter graduate school with the intention of becoming a college professor it was to Father he went for advice, not to his own father. (I do sometimes wonder if Father could possibly have advised him not to conform to Mr. Mercer's wishes in such a matter. It would have been almost unthinkable on Father's part, and yet I do believe that it must have been Father's advice that Alex followed.) And I recall that when I wished to marry the girl in Chattanooga whom I was in love with during the War, it was to Alex that my father went for support in preventing me. Alex declined even to speak to me about the matter at the time and told Father that he would not. But he did tell me all about it several years later. Moreover, when I finally left home after the War and came off to Manhattan, it was to Alex of course that Father applied in his efforts to try to understand why I had found it necessary to leave.

Despite the periods of intimate exchanges between him and Father it was Alex and I who remained steadfast friends all through the years. After I left home his letters to me came much more regularly than those from any of my family. Important news of the family was much more likely to reach me first from Alex than it was from anyone else. It was therefore in no sense surprising that it was he who kept me informed of Father's and Betsy's and Josephine's behavior during the year following Mother's death.

Alex was uneasy of course from the very first about how my sisters might react to any new relation between Father and his and Mother's women friends. I paid little attention to the alarms he sounded. It was only when Alex's wife protested, at the time when the three of us were riding in the back seat of the undertaker's limousine, that I understood what it was Alex was saying. It was Frances Mercer's disingenuous tone that made me understand. I saw that she harbored the same forebodings that he did. Later during the funeral visit home and again during my next visit, only a few weeks later, Alex pointed out the danger once again. I began to wonder if there was something about Father that Alex perceived and that I didn't. On one of these occasions Alex said to me explicitly that he thought he understood certain elements in my sisters' affection for Father that I did not. Since I sometimes trusted Alex's observations about people more than I did my own— about the very conventional Memphis people, that is—I listened to him this time. My sisters loved Father so deeply, he told me, that they were apt to be made jealous of those widow friends he and Mother had had. Knowing what our family life was like, this seemed unreasonable to me, and it seemed that possibly Alex was not telling me all that was on his mind. On the other hand, Alex's observations were to be trusted more than my own *only* with regard to the truly conventional Memphis people. He sometimes made the mistake of forgetting how strange the Carver family seemed to him when he first knew us.

Alex knew as well as I that during the many, many years that Mother lived the life of an invalid and did not go out socially, Father had continued to attend all kinds of evening parties. And during that time there had never been a whisper of scandal. Alex must have been told as often as I how Father and Mother would frequently stay up half the night after such parties, with Father repeating every bit of party conversation, just to amuse Mother, and replaying, so to speak, every hand of bridge. While they enjoyed themselves thus Mother would be sitting up in bed, drinking cup after cup of hot chocolate which Father had made repeated trips to the kitchen to prepare. And then on the following day he would be up early and off to his office while she frequently slept the entire morning, exhausted, she liked to say, by the thought of the party she had not even attended.

About my sisters Alex certainly understood much less than I. In his words of praise for them concerning how attentive they were to Father, he unknowingly revealed to me that Father *didn't* confide in him what it was they talked to him about in the Club dining room or at the downtown restaurants. I think Alex didn't at all suppose how often Betsy and Jo were making Father miserable even when they were well over fifty years old—that is, by going on at such great length about the men they might yet marry or the affairs they were ostensibly having (it was only when Mother was not present that they went at this subject in the most intense way), or embarrassing him by their youthful costumes and with the slang they evidently picked up from young men they sometimes went out with—phrases like "no way" and "way out." Yes, when Alex Mercer spoke to me about Betsy's and Jo's love for Father, I reflected silently to myself: Ah, Alex, you and your provincial Memphis love for a *simple* truth! He did not dream, I told myself, that simultaneous with their love and admiration which they so often expressed for Father they were silently experiencing emotion of the very opposite kind. Or perhaps Alex did dream of that paradox and, like me, could not bring himself to speak of it to me or even acknowledge it to himself.

5

I REMEMBER THAT by the time I was in my early
twenties there was no one but Alex to whom I could confide
my feelings. This was especially true with regard to my feelings about the unhappy end to the great love affair of my
youth. I remember telephoning Alex from Chattanooga, which
is where my dear Clara Price lived—lived with her family of
course, in a splendid Tudor-style house atop Lookout Mountain. Both times that I called Alex from Chattanooga I began
by saying that I could see no reason to go on living without
Clara. He kept me on the phone for thirty minutes, telling me
all the other things I did have to live for, which of course was
what I wished to hear. During that same year, on a visit back
to Memphis from Chattanooga, I once actually wept in Alex's
presence over the loss of that same girl. My motive for revealing all this about myself now is simply to be able to say that
I have never known another person I could have faced again
after those hysterical telephone calls I made to him and after
my tearful performance in his presence when I was home a

few days later. (This was in 1941. I was in the Army at the time and stationed at Fort Oglethorpe, Georgia, which is nine miles below Chattanooga and Lookout Mountain.) But in the case of Alex, it was relatively easy to face him again. And it was not merely his sympathy that was consoling—more, rather, the feeling he could give one that it was indeed his own reserved behavior that was outrageous and not one's own self-pitying outbursts.

But all of this reminds me that during the intermission between my sisters' calls, that grim Sunday twilight, and before I had made my decision to go to Memphis next day, I found myself thinking of Alex Mercer and Clara Price, as well as of my father. I sat there for a time in the loggia of my as yet unlit Manhattan apartment not bothering to put on the lights or to return to my desk, back in my study. I knew of course that the second call would come soon. And even if I had not been anticipating that second call from Josephine, still the first had raised enough forebodings and memories to keep me from returning to the desk work that had been interrupted. I sat in the dark by the telephone and remembered what I thought was forgotten: old feelings of resentment against Father for his interference in my romance with that girl in Chattanooga, my wonderful Clara Price. Did Clara Price come into my mind at that time only because she shared her Christian name with old Mrs. Clara Stockwell? I couldn't be sure, but several episodes relating to Clara came back to me.

It was to Alex Mercer of course that Father went in support of his efforts to interfere with my plans to marry. There are two memorable details in Alex's later account to me of that consultation with my father. One was that this occasion was the first on which Father ever actually went to Alex Mercer's house. They had been friends and confidants for a good many years by this time, but there had never been anything so personal as this. Alex had married when still very young and lived with his wife, Frances, and their two small children (the first two of his flock) in an unattractive little bungalow near Memphis State University. They live there to this day, with the other children that have followed. Father had telephoned in advance before making the visit. I suppose he elected to go to the house for the talk because of the private nature of the subject for discussion, but also because it was a Saturday afternoon and he reckoned that Alex would not be at his University office. He had telephoned in advance but was later in arriving than Alex had counted on. Perhaps Father had difficulty in finding the house since it was not in a part of town that he knew well or would have liked going to.

Alex was watching from a front window when he saw his friend Mr. George pull up to the curb and step out of the car. He had been watching there for quite a while and he wondered that, being so late as he was, Father moved as slowly as he did once he had stepped out of the car. By this time of life Father was dressed in the Memphis style he had adopted. It was early spring, and he was wearing what Alex called a Stetson hat (though Alex knew exactly nothing about clothes of a Memphis style or any other) and he wore a belted polo coat. (That much Alex would have been able to identify correctly.) As Father came along the brick entry walk from the public sidewalk he kicked aside clusters of dead leaves that had lain there since the previous autumn and had been matted together by the snows and rains of winter. Father carefully brushed these dirty leaves aside with the highly polished toe of his tan, wing-tipped shoes. And this gesture made a wounding impression on Alex, I think. He attributed Father's hesitation as he came along to the unpleasant necessity of approaching a house where people didn't bother to rake the dead autumn leaves until spring. (This was only a few days before Easter.) Such observations did not, I think, make Alex wish to become the sort of man who *did* rake his leaves in the fall of the year but he did regret submitting a man like Mr. George Carver to his own less conventional ways. He imagined that Father, as he approached, seemed uneasy and that the old gentleman felt himself out of place in such a tacky bungalow neighborhood as this.

What Alex did not realize was that in all probability Father was simply dreading this interview he had arranged and was kicking the leaves absentmindedly. My father was of course coming to ask Alex whether or not he thought it would be dishonorable for him, as my father, to go to Chattanooga and talk to Clara Price's father about Clara and me without first telling *me* he was going to do so. And very right Father was to dread the interview too. Because Alex told him, as Father no doubt knew he would, that it *would* be dishonorable for him to do so. And yet despite Alex's answer Father did go to Chattanooga to see Mr. Price. He went the very next day and he went without consulting me, as he doubtless knew he would do regardless of Alex's opinion.

Alex didn't tell me about any of this at the time. And neither at that time nor afterward did he tell Father about the call he had from me that day. The fact was that during the long interval between Father's advance telephone call and his actual arrival at Alex's front door, he, Alex, had received one of my own long-distance calls from Chattanooga (in the course of which I had declared I could see no reason to go on living if I did not have the love of Clara Price). Alex Mercer's silences could be wonderful. He did not, as I have said, tell my father about my call and did not of course tell me till many years later about Father's expected visit. He did not even tell me about it when at Christmas of that year, by which time Clara had allowed herself to be sent to South America by her father, I had come home to Memphis, had come to weep openly in Alex's presence and to tell him that I had good reason to believe that I was losing my mind.

With reference to losing my mind, I told Alex then how just two days after our last telephone conversation I had got off a streetcar on Market Street, in Chattanooga, and had thought I saw my father going into the main entrance of the old Patton Hotel. I told Alex how I ran after the man, calling out first: "Father! Father!" And then: "Mr. Carver! Mr. George Carver!" But the man had passed quickly through the revolving door without looking back. Then, running at top speed, in my long enlisted man's overcoat and in my heavy government-issue shoes, I followed him inside, sure that it was my father I had seen entering. But he was nowhere to be seen in the lobby. I inquired at the desk if there were a "George Carver of Memphis" registered there. And I felt sure the desk clerk was lying to me when he assured me there was not. Alex took my hand when I told him about all this and held it in a firm grasp. But he was unwilling, because of Father's confidence, to say anything that might explain or interpret my "hallucination."

OF COURSE IT would all become clear to me in later years when I was a little more sophisticated. At some point the mystery is removed from young people's eyes. At last they understand how it is that adults have always behaved with them. As I sat alone in my Manhattan apartment waiting for the second call from Memphis during that twilight hour my head was full of such adult understanding. For me the mystery had been removed many long years before, and none of it mattered much any more. I would soon be an old man myself, wouldn't I? And my sisters would even sooner be called old ladies, if they could not already be called that. I sat and listened to the sound of the traffic ten stories below and thanked God for the city's hum that seemed to shut out all human noise. Even when the call came from my other sister I didn't really listen to her voice. I knew too precisely what she was going to say, which was of course precisely what the first sister had said. While Josephine spoke, I continued to think of my old flame Clara Price and what she had been like when I first saw her at the age of twenty-three. It would be a mistake on my part to try to give any real impression of what Clara seemed like to me at that age. No one can give an adequate picture of the person who has captured his imagination as Clara captured mine. The important thing would be to show the effect she had on me and the effect our final breaking off and the role my father played in that breaking off had on the rest of my life. It doesn't matter whether Clara was beautiful or merely striking-looking, whether she was a sensitive and gifted artist or a young woman of great spirit and force, someone who inspired the best in me or made me feel humble in her presence. Whatever she was like, no other girl ever delighted me as she did, and she must remain for those who never knew her simply the girl in Chattanooga I was beyond any question very profoundly in love with during that first year of the War, must remain simply the girl whom my father, for needs and reasons of his own or out of a general confusion about the role he was entitled to play with regard to his children's selection of their mates, succeeded in preventing me from marrying. I have stated already that I was then stationed at Fort Oglethorpe, Georgia, just a few miles south of Chattanooga. I was only an enlisted man at the time, but since this was before the United States actually entered the War, I kept a room in a grimy old rooming house in downtown Chattanooga and spent my weekends there. To a more recent generation it will seem strange that I was drafted into the Army before we were in the War, but the draft did exist before we had got into actual hostilities, and when I registered

in Memphis as a conscientious objector, stating on the form
that I would never perform the act of killing merely because
I was ordered to do so by officeholders in the Federal Govern-
ment or by their appointees in the Army, I was immediately
ordered to report for induction at the Reception Center, Fort
Oglethorpe, Georgia. The girl who was clerk in the draft
board office and with whom I had had a number of dates
during my high school years told me that she had sent in my
draft form along with the others because she thought that by
"act of killing" I was referring to some "Act of Congress."
And she didn't quite understand what I meant. This was *so*
like a certain type of Memphis mentality to do just that! I
could not even bring myself to protest. I could only regard
it as a kind of grotesque joke. "At least this will get me out
of Memphis," I said to myself. After all, my "conscientious
objection" did not come out of any firm and profound philosophical position. How was one to know whether or not one
should fight in the big abstraction that all modern wars are?
What had it to do with the clutter of daily life in a place like
Memphis? Or Nashville? Or Knoxville? Or Chattanooga? Or
even Huntingdon or Huxley or Thornton? I had written
down my objections to the act of killing almost as a reflection of my mood on that particular day. The whole thing was,
to some degree, like an unreal joke. But the War itself seemed
an unreal and obscene joke in those days before we were
really in it—or seemed so to those of us who didn't remember
the First War. And once I was installed at Fort Oglethorpe
and assigned permanently to the Reception Center Headquarters, then peacetime Army life seemed even more unreal
and more ridiculous than all the rest of the cluttered-up,
bourgeois life I knew in Tennessee towns and cities.

The atmosphere in my rooming house in Chattanooga was
far more depressing than that in the canteen and in the bar-

racks at Fort Oglethorpe. Life "out at the Post" was actually quite cheerful with the games and the drilling and the few short hours of work and, after work, the long hours of freedom in Chattanooga and on Lookout Mountain. It was from that rooming house on Saturdays that I was able to do my book hunting in the old parts of town—on Saturdays and on late afternoons during the week. I think there was not a secondhand junk shop whose premises I did not frequent regularly or a private sale of household goods that I did not attend (in order to buy books that happened to be there). Since Fort Oglethorpe was in Georgia, it was on eastern time, and it was also on daylight saving time during the summer. All of this meant that when it was five o'clock at the Post, it was but three o'clock in Chattanooga proper.

What a wonderful summer it was for Fort Oglethorpe soldiers—for both officers and men—that last summer and autumn before we entered the War. After three-thirty it wasn't easy to find a free table in the Read House coffee shop or in the beer parlor adjoining it. And I suspect it was rare for there to be a vacancy in the rooms upstairs, either at the Read House or at the Patton Hotel, a few blocks away. The girls in Chattanooga during those times were, like Hemingway's girls in Milan, the most patriotic citizens in the whole town—not only the girls in the Read House beer parlor or in a dozen other similar joints and in the very streets of the town, for that matter, but girls of a superior kind too who were to be met at church suppers and at the U.S.O. and some of them also in the rooms upstairs at the Read House. I had not, myself, very much acquaintance with any of those girls except as they were known to me on the arms of other soldiers who were my friends. But I listened very carefully to what those friends of mine told me about their girls. There was a very handsome soldier in our own Headquarters Company, a rather roughneck of a fellow when we went into town, given to brawling and heavy drinking, though on the silent side when out at the Post—except that he liked sometimes to talk to me. He was of a decidedly dark complexion and with black hair that was thick and extremely oily. I believe he was said to be half Cherokee Indian. He hailed from upper East Tennessee and spoke in flat accents that it was sometimes difficult for the rest of us to understand. But we envied him his exploits with women at the Read House. He told me once how he woke one Sunday morning in a narrow little room on the top floor of the hotel and knew almost immediately that the good life was over for him. He had been "all liquored up" the night before. He could not remember anything after leaving the Post. But he could tell instantly by the way a strange young woman seated at the hotel room's dressing table was humming to herself as she brushed her hair that she and he had got married before the past evening was over.

The point, however—the sad point—in my telling all this is that I had no part in such soldierly adventures or in that free life on the town which the other soldiers from Fort Oglethorpe were enjoying. I imagine that the truth is, I was not temperamentally suited for it. Yet it seemed to me even then that my lack could be blamed somehow and to some degree on that removal my father had made from Nashville to Memphis. By the other soldiers I was regarded tolerantly as a bookworm. I was teased about this a good deal at the Post, but once we were in town I was allowed to go my way in peace. In this sense the Army was better for me than my college years at Southwestern had been. There I had been bored to distraction by fraternity brothers—that is, after my father had prevailed upon me to join a fraternity. And because I would not as an undergraduate commit myself to attending some law school afterward, Father took no interest in my good grades there. When Mother sang my praises with regard to my good scholarship, he would say: "Yes, yes. He *is* bookish." He didn't ever, as a matter of fact, like for me to exhibit special knowledge on any subject. He had to that extent taken on the Memphis coloration. He didn't mind my collecting books but never liked my making reference to what was inside those books. Moreover, almost at once after arriving at Chattanooga, I became involved in the secondhand book world there, buying books that turned up in the junk shops along Market Street and of course at sales of private estates. It was in such places that one used to discover first editions—for a quarter or fifty cents. I soon had rare, musty old books stacked under my bunk in the barracks and all about my room in the rooming house. Then there was my other interest, too: the Civil War battlefields around Chattanooga —Chickamauga, Missionary Ridge, Lookout Mountain, and even Stone River less than a hundred miles away. (I even went down to Atlanta one weekend.) Of course I collected books about those battles but also I spent hours on the battlefields themselves, studying the monuments and the markers for the positions of both armies. I did not realize at this time, of course, what a dreary preoccupation it was I had drifted into. I had not realized it in college and had not realized it in high school, where it all began. But I was aware of and felt some shame over the fact that I had long since become more concerned with the value of the physical books themselves than with what was inside them. I did not speculate on how and why this had happened, though it would be easy to do so now.

BUT SUDDENLY THERE came a change and an awakening for me. It came almost in one moment, it seems to me now. I had ridden on the Incline Railway to the top of Lookout Mountain, planning to walk about in the park and see what evidence there was, if any, of the skirmish that had taken place there between Union and Confederate troops. My mind, you see, was all on that other war, not the war I was about to take part in. I was participating not in the life of people around me but in that of people who were now in the land of the dead. It was there I had temporarily taken refuge. It may be that I actually yearned to join those who were dead, but certainly I was not aware of the yearning and did not speculate on the possibility at the time. I kept my thoughts on known facts of battles and skirmishes. And that is where my thoughts were when I stepped off the Incline Railway and passed out through the covered walkway toward the mountaintop park. It was just as I came out that I caught my first glimpse of Clara Price, leaning against one of the rustic posts beside the entrance. And I cannot resist observing now that it would be there six months later that she and I saw each other for the last time at the end of our love affair. At that first glimpse we had of each other we nodded and smiled precisely as though we were meeting by appointment. I pretended I had stopped to ask directions of her, and she pretended to believe that was my only purpose. We spent that whole late autumn afternoon together, walking about the park and along the West Brow of the Mountain. She had come down to the Incline from her father's house to see her sister off to town, and she did not return home until I took the Incline car back down the Mountain at nine o'clock.

That Clara should respond to me so openly and easily as she did on that first meeting was not unusual in wartime. It was in the line of duty, so to speak, for young ladies and for girls of all kinds to talk to soldiers who were lonely and far away from home and to walk with them in whatever park was at hand. Little did Clara Price know the deadness of my existence or the need I had of her—not that day. But she would soon know. Surely no life was ever so quickly and completely transformed by love as mine was. Within a few days my reading was no longer confined to books on Southern military history. I gave up visiting junk shops and attending sales of household goods. I was reading poetry again and even writing it, after a fashion. It did not matter to me of course whether or not it was good poetry I wrote. The "feeling" was everything. It seemed to me I was alive again—really for the first time since leaving the little girl with the Dutch bob on Franklin Pike at Nashville. Within a few weeks I was spending Saturday nights not in my rooming house but in the guest room of Clara's parents' house up there on the West Brow Road of Lookout Mountain.

Her family was well disposed toward me from the beginning. They were all of them—the entire family—great readers. Clara and I made use of their library all through the fall and winter months that followed. We read aloud to each other from the volumes of Keats and Shelley which I found there and from an elaborately decorated volume of Vachel Lindsay's poetry. In every book there would be at least one four-leaf clover that Clara had found and placed there to be pressed between the pages. She had a remarkable visual perception, especially for four-leaf clovers, and in the early fall we could walk scarcely twenty feet on the lawn without her stooping to pick one—never interrupting the flow of our talk. Sometimes I borrowed books from her family's library and took them back to the Post to read. I would find it very touching when I came upon a pressed clover leaf and would sit on my bunk gazing off at the barracks ceiling instead of reading the book before me.

Even after the autumn weather began to turn cold, Clara and I would frequently take a book outside to read. As we looked for a good spot to settle ourselves in she would often stoop to pluck a clover that was still green amidst the coarse winter grasses. In the Prices' library the volume of Vachel Lindsay was the most recent book of poetry except for a small pink paperback anthology edited by Harriet Monroe— of the kind one used to find at Woolworth's. We read some in that too. At first I was interested only in the bindings of the books and the paper and print and in the date of publication. But after Clara read aloud to me one evening from Harriet Monroe's anthology, I began, myself, reading poetry again for the first time since I had left school. One evening a week before her birthday in September I had found in the Market Street Bookshop, a very prettily made volume entitled *A Garland of Christmas Verse*, edited by S. C. Mayle. I bought it for Clara and persuaded the book dealer to "gift-wrap" it, though he found it hard to scrape up such wrappings in that dirty and cluttered old shop of his. Later I rode the Incline Railway up the Mountain of course and walked under a starry winter sky the half mile to Clara's house. Her parents, who were, so it seemed to me, old enough to be her grand-parents—being much older certainly than my own parents— had already retired to their rooms for their evening of read-ing. Her sister, who was just going out, greeted me at the front door. Clara was waiting for me always in the library. When I came in and at once handed her the book she blushed and smiled at me in delight, like a little girl receiving her first present at her birthday party. "Am I to open it now?" she asked.

"Of course you are. It's a pre-birthday present," I said.

She tore off the paper with real anticipation, I felt. She peeped inside the book to the selection of very old and little-known Christmas verse. Then almost before I knew it she had thrown her arms about my neck and kissed me so lovingly that I made an effort to draw her further into a possibly less visible corner of the room. But she laughed at my effort.

"What do we care who sees us?" she asked. But I managed to lead her to the nearby couch and there returned her kiss many times over. Finally she held me a little away from her and looking directly into my eyes she said softly, "Some night I want you to go with me to my room, Phillip." Of course I went with her that very night, and from that time we were truly lovers and imagined ourselves bound to each other for life.

Below the west front of the Prices' house, overlooking the wide spread of Sequatchi Valley below, there was a small stream, and in the wintertime there was a considerable flow of water over the rocks there, constituting a miniature water-fall and cascade down the steep escarpment of the mountain-side. On the coldest days Clara and I used to sit beside the stream and watch the swift passage of the transparent water. We delighted in it especially when there were inlets of ice along the edges, and the water flow seemed to have to make a great struggle not to freeze altogether. When the stream was half frozen like that along the edges the sun would some-times come out and the surface of those myriads of icy little inlets would glisten like so many pieces of broken mirror. I don't know how many times or for how long each time we sat watching the ice and water like that. At least a half dozen times during the winter, I believe. But once especially I re-member finding Clara already there at the creekside when I came up from Fort Oglethorpe on a Saturday afternoon. I had brought her an armful of presents that day. I had come to Lookout by way of Chattanooga, which was necessary since I came on the streetcar all the way from the Post, and I had stopped by two used-book stores and at other shops, too, to find things that I knew would delight her. Besides two pretty little first printings of American editions of Swinburne and of Ernest Dowson, I had bought three other small presents—a fragile Chinese jar full of potpourri, only six inches high or less, a lavender-and-mustard-colored silk scarf, a gold pin set with infinitesimal rubies, the last of which cost at least half my year's Army pay. Clara opened the presents with consummate care, one by one, and after each opening we embraced. She would throw back her head and laugh with delight and then we would exchange long embraces, sitting beside each other in our heavy winter clothes on the creek bank.

She was the first person, perhaps the only person, I ever bought presents for. Her joy and delight were my reward, and it pleased me that she never responded by making any sort of present to me in return.

ONLY A FEW weeks before Clara left me and was sent off to South America, I had made a quick trip to Memphis, primarily to see my mother, who was experiencing one of her periods of total withdrawal from the life around her. I spent several hours alone with Mother, but I did not talk to her about Clara. Once, however, when she was at her dressing table fingering idly a tray of jewels of varying worth as well as other trinkets and keepsakes, I looked over her shoulder, and there in her tray I spied a very pretty gold pendant in the shape of a four-leaf clover. It was delicately made and had a smaller clover leaf etched inside each of the four lobes, and it was attached to a double gold chain with links so extraordinarily small that together the twisted chains seemed almost a string of gold mesh. Because of the association it immediately had for me back on Lookout Mountain, I found it breathtakingly beautiful. I had never seen Mother wear it on her person, and I felt almost that she had placed it in her dressing-table tray in order that it should catch my eye. Yet

I knew of course that in reality my seeing it was merest chance.

I asked Mother to let me examine it and told her that the girl I was "seeing" in Chattanooga had a special penchant for four-leaf clovers. Perhaps despite myself I was actually hinting that she give it to me, but I was more aware of being carried away by the coincidence. Mother at once pressed it upon me, urging me to give it to the girl I was "seeing." She looked at me rather tenderly, I felt, and said: "It is something I have always meant to dispose of, to give away. But it is not the kind of thing either of your sisters likes, and your friend is just the person to have it. I should tell you it is something given to me by someone I loved very much before I met your father. He died—the person I'm speaking of—he was killed in an accident. He died in a fall from a horse. It has made me dislike horses ever since. I suppose I kept this little pendant out of sentiment for a good many years, though I have none about it now. I have always kept it hidden from your father and have sometimes even felt guilty about it. But I have no sentiment about it now. I am afraid I have no sentiment about anything any more. You will do me a favor to take it off my hands. Your friend is just the person I would have liked to give it to." Then she insisted that I should take it to a jeweler and have one of the tiny links in the chain repaired and have the gold pin from which it hung either straightened or replaced.

Since I did want the ornament to be perfect when I presented it to Clara I took it to a Chattanooga jeweler to have the repairs made. When next I went to Lookout Mountain I told Clara that I would have a special present for her on the following weekend. I saw tears come into her eyes when I told her, but at the time I thought this only an indication of what a responsive and warmhearted girl she was. I did not know then that my father had already been to Chattanooga to see her father (I believed I had only imagined seeing him enter the Patton Hotel) and that Clara already knew she was going to allow herself to be sent away to Brazil without even saying goodbye to me. When I rode the Incline Railway up to see her that next weekend with the repaired pendant in my pocket, she was gone, and even her parents and her sister refused to see me. In the following months I felt on some days I was going to die from heartbreak and I only wished to die. But on other days I only hated Clara for treating me so and for allowing herself to be so treated. But no matter what my mood was, I kept the little pendant and didn't return it to Mother at once. When I did try to return it a few weeks later, she refused to accept it. "Wait a while, Phillip," she said, "and give it to someone else."

"I could never do that," I said.

"Don't be so hard to please, son," she said. "Sometimes the second choice is better than the first would have been." She didn't understand at all, or at least she wouldn't. But of course in a way I was glad to have to keep the little gold clover leaf. In fact, I was never without it afterward. I was careful never to let anyone see it, but I even took it with me when at last I went overseas. I kept it hidden in a concealed compartment of my wallet, never taking it out to look at even when I was alone. If anyone should have discovered it there, I was prepared to tell them it was something my mother had given me for good luck before I left to go overseas. I thought that would sound plausible and would not be altogether untrue. But, as it turned out, I never had to explain or had to offer the not altogether untruth to anyone, not even to Alex Mercer.

Alex was shipped overseas at about the same time that I was. He was an officer, of course, and was stationed in France at General Headquarters immediately after Paris fell. I stayed with him whenever I was there on three-day passes, and we had some fine times together. I think either of us would have been too timid to explore Paris and enjoy it as we did if the other had not been present. Alex had a more comprehensive knowledge than I of what there was to be enjoyed, but I think perhaps what he actually delighted in most was eating in the Army cafeterias that were supplied by the U.S. Army but were staffed by French cooks. I had been in England for a while first, and after shabby wartime London, everything in liberated Paris looked prosperous, and the civilians were very well dressed—just the way one expected Parisians to be whether liberated or living under the Occupation. One day we were walking along the Rue de Rivoli and saw a familiar figure ahead of us. At first I thought it was someone I knew, and then after a moment I realized it was Gertrude Stein. Somehow there was nothing surprising about seeing her. Alex and I had the same reaction. It was as inevitable as seeing the Eiffel Tower in Paris. We introduced ourselves to her, and she of course invited us to tea at her house in the Rue Christine. She was very kind to us, and we sat in her living room for an hour, looking at her pictures and talking about Anthony Trollope. Finally Alex introduced the name of the poet Allen Tate, who had been in Paris after the First War and who later lived in Memphis for a time. She remembered him well and remembered how much she had disliked his wife, Caroline Gordon. We had known Allen and Caroline in Memphis, and Alex undertook to defend Caroline in a good-natured way. Here we were in this Paris salon in the middle of the War, talking cozily about people we knew in Memphis. I remember reflecting to myself how like Alex it was, how like most Memphians it was, even in such a time and such a place as this, finally to reduce even such a conversation as this to gossip and small talk about people in Memphis.

While I was there in Paris I found myself as usual think-ing about my father. He had been too old to go to the First War. He was married and had four children by then. It seemed sad to me that he had not been able to come to Paris. He would have loved the way people dressed, and it might have changed his style permanently. I myself went to Paris at every opportunity, though I was never stationed there. But the last time I went was just before my outfit received orders to go up to the Battle of the Bulge. I never actually got as far as the front lines, but I thought certainly I was destined to be killed there, and when I was in Paris on my last three-day pass before going up, I gave Alex a little snap purse I had bought which contained the gold pendant and a watch that had belonged to my maternal grandfather in Nashville, as well as two or three other keepsakes of less value. You see, I couldn't bring myself to throw the pendant away or have it picked off me by some German, and so I lumped it in with those other things just in case anyone opened it before my mother did. I told Alex to take it back to the States to my family if he went home before I did. I did not explain the contents because I knew of course that Alex would lay down his life before letting anyone open it before he handed it to my parents. As it was, the colonel of our regiment was dis-graced and sent home next week for favoring the athletes in our outfit and not making them do guard duty. And so we were never sent to the front because our colonel was such a rotter. Alex returned the purse to me a few weeks later with-out ever asking me, of course, what the contents were.

DURING THE SIX months of our love affair Clara Price and I explored the woods and ravines on that mountaintop where she lived, taking picnic suppers to the waterfalls even in very cold weather and to the mouth of the great cave. I must not say that our life during those two short fall and winter seasons was idyllic. Rather, it was a grand and glorious reality that I came upon out of the drabness of my life both before and afterward. And it was that which my father, that day when I saw him going into the Patton Hotel, had come to Chattanooga to destroy and succeeded in destroying. By December all of it was over. Clara had been sent away by her parents, and I had resumed my dreary hours in my rooming house. Then on December 7th of course the whole face of life changed. I was alone in my room on the Sunday afternoon when the news came that we were in the War. I gave notice to my landlady that night and went back to the Post. I knew my military life would be a somewhat more serious affair from then on. And a few days later I went into town and saw to having my books packed and shipped to my father's house in Memphis. Within three months I was sent to a training camp in New Jersey, and then overseas. I was in Europe for more than two years and never once had occasion to speak Clara Price's name or to hear it spoken. I returned to Memphis after the War and remained there for another two years without once hearing Clara's name mentioned. Memphis seemed to me then a province more foreign to that of Lookout Mountain than any place I had been stationed on the continent of Europe. In Memphis, after the War, I drifted from one small job to another, keeping all the books I continued to collect in an unused room above the garage. My mother and father still lived at that time in their old house at midtown.

ON AN EARLY, rather frigid November morning, two years after I returned from overseas, I climbed out of my bed in that house of my father's and left the house forever. I was heading that morning for my new life in New York City.

Within less than a year after I took that abrupt and secretive departure, Father would sell the house and move Mother and himself to the suburbs. It was before 6 a.m. when I got up and began packing my little bag and dressing myself, scarcely aware somehow of what it was I was doing—that is, that I was about to leave my parents' house without saying goodbye and without telling them where I was going. Perhaps it was because I felt it a shameful thing to be doing that I could not let my mind confront its reality. Perhaps even more shameful for me was the very fact of my running away from home like this, like a little boy in a storybook, when I was already a man of almost thirty with his college years and even his war years now well behind him. At my relatively mature age I was playing Peter Pan, going off to live amongst the Lost Boys and blaming it all on the incomprehensible machinations of my father. As I packed my things, scarcely more than I might have needed had I been setting out for an overnight trip, and put on my clothes—my ordinary, "everyday" clothes—it was as though someone else were dressing me and packing for me or at least as though I had no will of my own. I didn't feel consciously or explicitly that it was my sisters who were directing my actions but I did feel that I wasn't entirely acting on my own volition. Earlier that fall Betsy and Jo had made a visit to New York—something I believe they had never before done. In the past, and always afterward too, it had been their custom to go to Chicago for shopping and for enjoying the stimulation of a big city. (That is a preference people in Memphis used to have, whereas Nashvillians were apt always to go to New York.) When my sisters returned from that New York trip they talked for weeks of nothing else but Manhattan's being the cultural capital of the country. When on the strength of this and partly out of mere politeness I quite casually expressed the wish that I might someday go there to live and to establish myself in the rare-book business, Betsy very soon presented me with an airline ticket to the great city. And knowing my lethargy about such things, she offered to have her secretary make a reservation for me whenever I should decide to go.

Two days before my departure I telephoned her secretary and asked that favor. When the secretary called back to give me my schedule she said Betsy had requested that I come by her house on the morning I was to leave and have breakfast with her. And so on that morning I walked the two short blocks from Father's house to Betsy's and when I arrived Betsy had my breakfast waiting. We ate together in the tile-floored breakfast room. I expressed my shame to her at running away in this Peter Pan fashion. And I based my excuse on the fear that Father would talk me out of going. He had never hesitated to use all his cunning as a courtroom lawyer to persuade his children to follow the course he prescribed. I remember how Betsy closed her eyes on this occasion and placed her hand on mine. "Don't I know!" she whispered. "We've learned, Jo and I, that this is the only way to deal with him in these matters. But we'll make it all right with Father—and of course with Mother." I thought to myself even while she and I sat there over breakfast that it must have been much the same when Georgie left for the Army. She was so reassuring, however, that by the time I left her house I felt I had made the decision to go quite independently and needed to feel no shame about the unmanly manner of my leaving.

Yet on my way to Josephine's house, which was but another two short blocks away and from which I had been told that Josephine would drive me to the airport, I made further comparisons with their assistance in Georgie's escape to the Army and to his death—comparisons, that is, with my escape to New York and whatever would come after. Surely there were never daughters more devoted to a father than they. In a sense they had devoted their entire lives to him. Could it be, though, that they were more devoted to their brothers' well-being than to their father's? I knew of course that that was nonsense! Yet it seemed that where our interests were concerned they were willing to go against him surreptitiously. Betsy had driven Georgie to Fort Oglethorpe to volunteer in the Air Corps. (I was stationed in the Reception Center Headquarters at the time and saw the papers proving he was a volunteer, not a draftee.) Josephine for two days had lied to Father concerning Betsy's and Georgie's whereabouts. They were willing to assist Georgie even in his seeming determination to be killed in the War. And I do not know that in all their lives they ever did anything else so directly in opposition to Father's wishes—except, that is, for moving from under his roof and into their own separate houses. (I believe if they had moved together into one house, Father would not have been so offended.)

Josephine was waiting for me that last morning with a check that would support me during my first six months in New York and with a letter from a New York business acquaintance of hers, offering me a room on MacDougal Street, at a very decent rent. Moreover, when we sat together for a few minutes in the front living room of her house she promised me, in the most businesslike tones, that she not only would assist Betsy in making everything right with Father and in making poor Mother understand, but would undertake to have all my books packed up and sent on to me as soon as I had a place for them. Then she asked: "Is there anything else I can do?"

I am afraid I spoke earnestly, like a little boy: "I'll need more clothes than this"—holding up my little traveling bag. She seemed touched by my request and bent forward and kissed me on the cheek. I do think she saw me at that moment as a sort of miserable orphan child.

"You just send me a list, Phillip," she said. Then we went out and got into her car, and she drove me to the airport. On my flight to New York I found myself going over and over what I knew and remembered of both my sisters' unhappy experiences during the unhappy times of our removal from Nashville to Memphis. I suffered for them that morning as never before.

6

As I have indicated earlier, it was only a matter of a few weeks after Father left off dining with those old ladies that the picture changed entirely. There was to follow the period during which the old gentleman's nightlife would become something quite different. Along with everybody else concerned, I began hearing about it at once. And it was at once apparent that Betsy's and Josephine's anecdotes were no longer intended to be merely amusing. In fact it was at this point that one would almost certainly have expected that things would go sour for them. But of course go sour they did not. Instead, the new stories were meant by my two sisters to be not merely funny but, in their own words, "hilariously funny." These new stories of course were not about polite dinner parties with old widow-ladies but about Mr. George Carver's "stepping out," as Betsy and Jo so merrily termed it, "stepping out with youngish women of a very different sort." (The women were always referred to as "youngish women," and it was as though they had no names.) And according to Alex the new kind of stories were generally prefaced by the sisters with demands, so Alex wrote me, for the attention of a whole roomful of people, not merely the attention of that customary circle of close friends. It was then, moreover, that the audience would be promised that the upcoming anecdotes would be not merely funny but hilariously funny.

Betsy and Josephine now seemed to become ever more voracious in their demand for listeners. They seemed to want to tell the whole world. And it seemed, night after night, that as their stories became more outrageous the manner of narration become softer and more genteel, and yet at the same time somehow higher-pitched and more shrill. This, too, may be only a part of the standard Southern lady's style—the obvious discrepancy, that is, between the content and the manner of narration. The manner was such, according to Alex Mercer, that on some occasions it could make him, standing as he generally was on the periphery of their circle, break out either in a cold sweat all over or at least in goose bumps about his neck. (I cannot help identifying myself with Alex in this as in so many instances. I think I would have responded just as he did, because in some ways we are remarkably alike. When we were boys and young men together we seemed to be of very much the same temperament and sensibility, with our interests in the arts and with our aspirations toward all things intellectual. We suffered equally from the sometimes crude behavior of people around us. But Alex of course chose finally to remain there at home and become the sedate university professor at Memphis State, whereas I had to go off to Manhattan to pursue my interests as a "dedicated bookman"—that's Alex's learned phrase for me. The major difference between us now would seem to be that Alex continues to regard himself as of the same species and breed as that of people like my sisters and my father, and I on the other hand do not continue quite to regard myself so.) At any rate, there was apparently nothing those two sisters of mine did not know about our father's new nocturnal adventures and nothing so degrading or humiliating to the old man that they would not report on it to very large groups of people. And yet I must say that all the while, so far as one could put one's finger on it, they were altogether tolerant of Mr. George's new activities. They seemed to be applauding his every move. Their response to all his activities was really something wonderful for Alex Mercer to behold!

What they professed to know, moreover (and what they even told me in their letters that they knew), was more than once corroborated for Alex by his young son Howard. Howard was barely twenty-two at the time, but he was not an altogether unreliable lad. Alex and Frances's other four or five children are totally vague and unreliable young people. I do not know how such upright, precise and accurate people as Frances and Alex Mercer could have produced such a houseful of flaky young people. (The adjective is theirs, not mine.) But young Howard is not an entirely unreliable boy. He does have a certain taste for low life, however, and is given to frequenting the very small-time honky-tonks where my father's adventures were currently being observed. What young Howard Mercer reported to Alex coincided closely with what I was told by my sisters in their letters. In fact, since I received the reports from Alex and Howard almost simultaneously with the letters from my sisters and since I do not save letters or keep a regular journal—but only these very irregular notebooks—I cannot be sure in all instances from which source I received the information I am presently going to give.

First, though, there might seem to arise the question of how Betsy and Josephine Carver (ladies in their fifties by this time) knew about Father's new nightlife, knew about it in such detail as they did. But really the question is how could they *not* know, living as they still did in what Alex and I sometimes refer to as Memphis Old Town. In Memphis Old Town all things seem to be known to all people even if one does not attend church or does not frequent its bars and discotheques. One is apt, one way or another, to be acquainted with every priest and minister and with every bartender and maître d' in that small segment of Greater Memphis. It would not be much of an exaggeration to say that everybody there knows everybody else and knows everything that happens to everybody—especially after dark. This is of course the Memphis of my own and Alex's adolescence and early young manhood. Today this segment remains the same small, compact city it was then. Only it is surrounded now by the new sprawling metropolis known as Greater Memphis. One sometimes feels that there is actually a high wall separating the two cities and keeping the two populations from mixing. Alex's academic colleagues at Memphis State University speak to him of Memphis Old Town, so he says, as a sort of sacred or royal inner city which in effect they do not enter or approach except on their knees. They, those colleagues of his at Memphis State, live of course as Alex does nowadays in the less personal if happier world of present-day, modern Memphis—Memphis-outside-the-walls—whereas Betsy and Josephine chose long ago to reside on one of the old streets in the Central Gardens District, so called nowadays, which is the very heart of Memphis Old Town.

My sisters' two houses are only a few blocks apart on the very same street and are almost identical to each other except that the exterior walls of Betsy's house are of what we used to call Catholic-church-yellow brick and those of Josephine's house are of a wire-cut burgundy-colored brick. Each house has a front stair and a servants' stair and a bright sun parlor off the living room and a bright breakfast room off the dining room. They are very roomy houses, indeed, and are remarkably like the house our family had lived in before Father built the one-story house in the suburbs for his and Mother's old age. The roof of each of my sisters' houses is of a terracotta color, being made of course of tile. (I do fervently hope that the reader has not imagined until now that Memphis Old Town in any way resembles the Vieux Carré in New Orleans or any similar old section of Richmond or Charleston or Savannah.) Across the front of each house is a tile-floored porch (scrubbed or hosed every Saturday morning by a black yardman) and there is a screened-in side porch (fitted in somewhere behind the sun parlor or the breakfast room) and there is also a latticed back porch. That is to say, each house has most of the old-time accouterments and comforts. At the time I speak of, Betsy and Josephine had lived there in those houses very comfortably for a number of years, entirely independent of our aged parents but with much coming and going in both houses by friends and by old acquaintances of every conceivable sort. It is safe to say that there was little news of the town that did not reach them.

THE NIGHT SPOTS where my father was often seen during that second phase of his going out were not very far from my sisters' own neighborhood. Those night spots—or "dives," as my sisters liked to represent them—were not of course the lowest kinds of places. They were not the hangouts of gangsters and such. They were more in the nature of neighborhood bars, bars that might perhaps be termed "discotheques," bars, at any rate, with a certain area of the floor set aside for dancing. And whatever electric light there was, was kept always at a very low wattage. Further, these places were situated in the relatively safe section of Old Town.

There was actually nothing illegal about their existence or their mode of operation. Yet the decor and the general atmosphere were surely calculated to remind the clientele of the bad old days of Memphis speakeasies and to make this relatively tame clientele imagine for a little while at least that they had entered a dangerous, after-dark world, one which in fact scarcely exists in that part of the city.

But the very names by which those places go may in fact tell more about them than would any account I can give. My father, who in most people's minds had always represented the very epitome of domestic propriety, was seen at the Blue Moon, at the Yellow Parrot, at the Red Lantern. He appeared one autumn night at the Blue Moon in the company of one of those youngish women I have mentioned (nameless in all accounts, and ageless). He arrived at the place toward midnight with a party of six people, all of whom were about the same age as the youngish woman on his arm. It is hard to imagine either of my two stout sisters in such a place, and it is far more difficult to imagine Father there. But I do believe Betsy was present that night. Since I do not keep my old letters, any letter that I have already answered or do not intend to answer goes immediately into my wastebasket. But I recall very well the great detail in which Betsy described that evening at the Blue Moon and recall the special attention given to what everybody was wearing, particularly to how Father was got up. The old gentleman was dressed appropriately enough, Betsy thought, in a gray pin-striped suit, a striped tie, and a pale blue shirt with a button-down collar. Both my sisters always had a good deal to say about the appropriateness and inappropriateness of other people's dress. This may seem strange in the light of how it was they usually dressed themselves. But somehow one felt that their own attire could not and was not intended to be taken straight.

Rather, their own attire seemed offered as a criticism of how those about them dressed. Or so I understood it. It seemed a kind of cruel joke between themselves and the beholder if the beholder understood them correctly. But however critical they were of most other people in Memphis, both sisters had always admired Father's social graces and appreciated and acknowledged his general charm for women. I had often enough heard them remark that whatever other misconceptions he had about himself and about the world, the old gentleman did know what clothes became him. I had heard them say more than once that his sense of the right attire for any occasion was never-failing. For Betsy and Jo this was a great and important compliment they paid Father. And what I must confirm is that this man, my father, this Mr. George Carver, did care more about clothes than any other man of his very masculine character and temperament that I have ever been acquainted with there in Memphis or here in Manhattan or in any other place at all.

I recall that Betsy reported him dressed that night at the Blue Moon in a gray pin-striped suit, giving also the design of his tie and the style and make of his shirt. But her letter had quite as much to say about what other members of his party were wearing. The men wore formal evening dress of a "cheap, tacky sort," according to Betsy. Two of them were "resplendent" (Betsy's word) in midnight-blue tuxedos. A third man "sported" (Betsy's word again, of course) a maroon dinner jacket. All three of them were decked out in pleated-bosomed shirts with ruffled cuffs of course that extended several inches below the jacket sleeves. Betsy's condescension to these people fairly leapt from the pages of her letter and especially so of course when she turned her attention to the women. The three women in the party were all of them in form-fitting dinner dresses with low necklines and long sleeves. Very *comme il faut!* (The French phrase and the exclamation point are Betsy's, naturally.) It was, she wrote me, as though those women had read in some women's magazine (bought no doubt in a Memphis supermarket) just what they should wear at the kind of place where they had obviously been to dinner that night—that is, before slipping away for slumming at the Blue Moon. In Betsy's eyes, they were a "common and comical-looking lot." The women, moreover, were wearing identical corsages that must all have come from the same source—namely, from the wealthy Mr. George Carver. In fact, there was such a spirit of celebration amongst the members of the party that it seemed to be some- one's birthday! Champagne was brought to their table—a practice generally unheard of at the Blue Moon! Somebody in the party must have called in ahead of time and had it ordered for the occasion. (That would be Mr. George Carver, of course.) But probably, said Betsy on second thought, it wasn't anybody's birthday, after all. She specu- lated that before coming to the Blue Moon their friend Mr. George had taken them all to some expensive restaurant or even out to the Memphis Country Club. (Betsy hoped not *there!*)

The youngish woman on Father's arm as he entered and who was seated next him later at their table seemed to find everything he said highly amusing. In the dimly lit area re- served for dancing this woman slow-danced with Father— aged eighty-one, it will be remembered, this old man who had played double solitaire so many late evening hours with his wife, our mother, when that poor, dear woman couldn't sleep, and who had played duplicate bridge with the old widow-ladies in more recent times—danced rather endlessly with him, the youngish woman did, sometimes clinging to him and with her head resting on his shirtfront, sometimes standing away while they danced and gazing up into his old eyes. But all the while that they were dancing, the man in their party wearing the maroon jacket remained at their table with his eyes on Mr. George and his dance partner. This man himself was seen to dance with no one other than this particular youngish woman whenever Mr. George would return her to their table. At those times the man would take her straight back onto the floor and while he and she danced together quite conventionally and slowly as though they had had much practice dancing together they talked continuously and with seeming intimacy, shaking their heads, sometimes frowning, sometimes both of them bursting simultaneously into laughter.

My sister was able indeed to give a very full account of that evening. Several times, she reported, this couple went from the dance floor to the bar and had drinks there together. Meanwhile, our old father, abandoned by the other two couples of the party as well, sat alone at the big table on the edge of the dance floor. Betsy said he looked conspicuously lonely there, like a dejected clown. At last the man in the maroon jacket and the youngish woman in her long-sleeved dinner gown (perhaps they were a married couple, Betsy suggested) finished off their last drinks at the bar and together made their exit from the Blue Moon. They did so without paying a bill or saying good night to Father or to any of the rest of the party.

Presently Father, while the two remaining couples were dancing, made his own exit alone. He had not at any time during the evening seemed to be aware of his daughter's presence. As for Betsy and her escort, whose identity was not mentioned in her letter to me, they kept close to their table in a dark and remote corner. She, sometimes pitying Father's plight and sometimes snickering to herself at the absurdity of the position the old man had placed himself in, carefully kept herself out of his sight. But what seemed significant to me and to Alex Mercer, who knew every detail of the evening, was that in neither Betsy's letter nor Josephine's letter, which came in the following mail and which consisted mostly of *her* report of *Betsy's* report of the same evening—in neither report, that is—was there any expression of resentment or outrage at Father's pathetic and unseemly attentions to the "youngish woman." There was merely condescension and amusement. There was even considerable constraint shown. And this was what neither Alex nor I could at first understand.

There was something else, too, that I myself did not understand until a week later when Alex's letter giving his son Howard's account of the evening arrived. What I read between the lines of that letter, without knowing whether or not Alex himself understood it, was that the man escorting Betsy that night was none other than Alex's son Howard. And when that realization dawned upon me from some in-advertent coincidence between the two accounts, another realization of still greater significance dawned upon me also, in a most blinding light: It came to me then, what I had never suspected before, that the effeminate, middle-aged men my sisters presented to me and to my father were not the men who took them to these night spots. Their late-night escorts were probably all quite young men, young men of decidedly low character—paid escorts, that is, or at the very least escorts whose admission and bar tabs Betsy and Jo paid wherever they went for an evening.

I HAD BEEN used for a good many years to my sisters' writing me about anything that concerned our parents' wel-fare. It was always assumed by them that they knew best about what was best for the old people. Not infrequently their two letters, sent from their separate houses, arrived in the same mail. It was really as if they did not think I would believe what I heard from only *one* of them. It was as if the

second letter were composed merely for the purpose of cor-
roborating the first. (This is why I felt so certain that the
second telephone call would come that Sunday night.) Usually I smiled to myself over each letter—written in almost
identical script—and then with a shrug I would toss both letters into my wastebasket. And that is what I did when I had
read their two letters about Father's evening at the Blue Moon
and read their gratuitous promises to me to keep a careful,
kindly eye on him in the months ahead.

After reading these letters about the Blue Moon rather
perfunctorily, I did literally toss them into the basket beside
my desk. But before getting back to work at my desk on each
of those mornings I gazed out my apartment window at the
city skyline. What a different world Memphis was, I said to
myself on each occasion. And each time I reflected silently
but emphatically that this was indeed a special Memphis phenomenon! It was *so* like the way things *used* to happen there,
I told myself. It was except that one had to take into account
certain eccentricities of my two sisters that went beyond the
eccentricities of dress. I am referring to the fact of how it
was that Betsy happened to be at the Blue Moon that night.
This fact was that she and Josephine, two middle-aged spinsters no less, frequented such places quite regularly—the Blue
Moon, the Yellow Parrot, the Red Lantern. These were
places where working men and women—white-collar work-
ers mostly—hung out on Saturday nights, along with a few
young people of all social and economic levels. But my two
sisters imagined or pretended to themselves to imagine that
these places were the equivalent of the speakeasies and nightclubs that their generation had taken such pleasure in visiting
back during the early thirties. I don't know whether Betsy
and Jo told their middle-aged women friends where it was
they went on their late-night "dates," but they liked to drop

the names of those places in Father's presence and then go off into peals of laughter. What they did not tell Father and me of course was that the men who escorted them there were not the same as those who appeared at their side at whatever debutante parties they were still invited to at the Country Club—were invited to, that is, out of propriety as older members of the Memphis establishment.

The mention of these late-night "dates" of theirs was always a matter of embarrassment to me, even though I was not thinking of the same men that they had in mind. Even at the time of my mother's death I seldom went home for a visit without one or the other of them confiding in me about some love affair she had just concluded or about an affair she was contemplating in the near future. It was offensive to imagine either of them with one of those middle-aged effeminate men, but it might have been more so to think of them with one of their paid escorts. At any rate, the affair was always just over or just about to begin. It was never described as being current. And I never had any illusion about its reality, of course, which made it somehow seem the more embarrassing. While my sisters made me listen to these confidences we would look into each other's eyes and we would laugh as merrily as if there were perfect understanding between us.

I knew always that the affair referred to was pure fantasy but I do not know even now whether or not they knew I knew. I knew also, moreover, and knew almost as a certainty —as I have said already—that during their girlhood romances these two sisters of mine had remained virgins. Their romances had been of the most old-fashioned kind and would have been consummated only in the marriage bed. This certainty—or near certainty—made all the talk of their lurid, nonexistent, middle-aged love affairs at once more laughable and more painful to me. On some occasions, when well past

fifty, one or the other of the two would introduce me to a
male acquaintance and ask that question: What sort of husband did I think he would make for her? And always with
the same senseless admonition: "Of course you must not tell
Father about him!" And then straightway I would hear
Father being told about the very same suitor.

After their first letters about the evening at the Blue
Moon, a series of letters followed. These letters reported that
Father was seen not only at their "nightclubs" (though they
did not in their very first letters say expressly that they themselves were present; it was not till later that they went so far)
but also at a number of the Cotton Carnival balls, was seen
there at the Country Club or the University Club superbly
got up of course, in white jacket and dark trousers. At those
balls he not only was seen "attempting to dance" but was
observed "cutting in on" the eligible young divorcées who
are always present at those parties. My sisters observed, moreover, that at those parties he paid but little attention to the
old ladies of his acquaintance—friends of our dead mother's
—or even to the pretty young debutantes, in the case of
whom courtesy might have been the excuse.

My sisters' letters were not altogether identical of course.
There was enough variety in the reportage always to keep
me from dozing over the second letter or altogether ignoring
it. It was as if certain kinds of information had been allocated
to each sister. Betsy, in one of her letters, enumerated the
night spots (with precise addresses) and specified the Cotton
Carnival balls at which the old gentleman had been seen
"attempting to dance." Both sisters seemed fond of using that
phrase. No doubt it was because they both prided themselves
so on their own dancing. Even nowadays when their figures
—and especially their legs—have seemed to grow heavier
between one of my visits and the next, they still indulged
sometimes in dipping and twirling and occasionally even in a

tango if they could persuade the orchestra to play one. I learned this, you see, from their own disquisitions when I was at home and they were devoting themselves to confiding in me. Oftentimes when I was being confided in I would have to turn away or busy myself with a cigarette in order to hide my blushes or perhaps hide a sad smile at the thought of the spectacle the two of them must create on the dance floor of the Country Club or at one of those neighborhood night spots.

IT WAS ACTUALLY the recent letters from Betsy and Jo that seemed to keep me awake during the night before I took that Monday-morning plane to Memphis. Their recent letters had dealt mostly with similar evenings passed in places similar to the Blue Moon. And in those recent letters that came week after week there was the same tone of restraint and amusement and always a suggestion of complicity and conspiracy—if only by their never manifesting to me their actual presence in those places where Father and his parties turned up. Or not doing so, at least, until the very end. They clearly were, for all the suggestion of conspiracy, bent upon keeping me posted about whatever developments there might be. They seemed for the nonce wisely determined to indulge the old man in his folly.

It was, in fact, as if he were not an old man at all but a young man in the family, the son or the nephew which none of us would ever actually have, who must be allowed to have his youthful fling, must be allowed to sow his wild oats. And one could imagine that this was allowable because his middle-aged aunts knew the world and knew the young man would finally settle down and find some decent girl we could all accept. Their letters were consistently filled with rich, sometimes humorous, sometimes poignant details, mostly about

Father himself, about how elegantly but sensibly he was always turned out. My sisters found it really wonderful and gratifying somehow that he continued to dress with the same punctilious care he had always shown. And it quite delighted me that in all this they made no reference to our dead mother or to how it had always been she whose responsibility and special pride it was more or less to manage his wardrobe and make it possible for him so consistently to turn himself out in the splendid style he was known for.

I think it might be explained here that Father's elegance by this time was strictly a Memphis elegance and his fashion a Memphis fashion. This was a point I am sure my sisters did not grasp entirely. (They had lived in Memphis too long by then.) I think they did not realize that in Manhattan or even in Nashville or Knoxville or Chattanooga people on the street might have turned and stared at Father and remarked on the peculiar cut of his jacket and the width of his hat brim. Nevertheless, in Memphis he was elegance and fashion itself for a man of his standing in his generation. Any knowledgeable person in Memphis, especially on Front Street or on downtown Madison Avenue, could tell at a glance who Father's black tailor had been and what Father's station in Memphis life was.

But in those later letters from Betsy and Josephine there were other kinds of details about Father's appearance. After my decision to take the Monday-morning plane to Memphis and during that long night before I would set out, the various details of their accounts kept crowding into my mind. One night Father had arrived at the Yellow Parrot with the usual sort of "youngish woman" on his arm and his crook-cane on his other. It was a cane he carried and made use of only when he was having one of his bouts with neuropathy. He stopped in the doorway and turned his freshly shaven old face first one way and then the other, as if scanning the whole wide, ill-lit room for a table. His daughter Josephine, who was present that night, watched him with some amusement as he paused there. She knew all too well how bad his sight was, even through the thick lenses of his horn-rimmed spectacles. He looked, she wrote me, vigorous and alert, towering above other men who were nearby. He looked altogether in command of the situation. And yet Josephine knew that except for those tables immediately around him and close to the doorway where he stood, he could not actually distinguish which tables were occupied and which were not. But Jo perceived that he was doing what she had so often seen him do—what we *all* had so often seen him do—in situations where he was not perfectly in command. That is, he was brazening it out. He was not giving in even to the smallest defeat. He simply stood still and waited for events to develop in his favor. He waited not patiently, not resignedly, but with decided confidence. Presently his female companion of that evening walked ahead of him in the direction of an empty table. And then Mr. George stepped aside and allowed several other couples with whom he and his woman friend had arrived to pass ahead of him. He followed at some distance and then all at once, midway across the room, the old man halted abruptly, jabbed his cane at the floor, and for an indeterminate time remained on the spot with his eyes closed and the weight of his long body pressing down on the cane. It seemed to Josephine like a matter of five minutes—though of course it wasn't so long, I suppose—that he remained standing there. And although the old man's daughter knew that he was suffering one of his terrible seizures of neuritic pain in his left foot and lower leg, the most that she could do, seated at the table with her "date," was to turn her head away from the awful sight. My other sister, in her letter which followed very soon, reporting events as Josephine had described them to her, said that of course Josephine's heart went out to him but that she knew too well that he would be humiliated and outraged if she had come forward to assist him.

Yet a quarter of an hour later Father was on the dance floor, "attempting to dance" to the deafening disco music. And when the seizure of pain came on him now a second time, his partner, out of embarrassment no doubt, simply turned her back on him and stood there a moment, staring off at the table where their friends were. Then presently she rushed off to the table and sent one of the youngish men in their party to look after Father and to bring him his cane. Meanwhile, she and the other woman of the party, with their heads lowered—again apparently out of embarrassment—and having gathered up their belongings at the table, now hurried off toward the entrance door. Perhaps they waited outside for the men to join them, but one could not be certain, said Josephine, they had not abandoned their escorts altogether.

It was these moments of failure with his "youngish women" that Betsy and Josephine described most graphically. Perhaps it was his repeated failures that made them feel that there was no need for resentment or interference on their parts. Moreover, if the kind of woman he was in pursuit of did not actually please them, at least they must have felt such women were no immediate threat to present arrangements—to Father's status, that is, as a widower. They professed, in their letters, to be mystified as to why Father insisted on going to "dance places" when he had such difficulty in dancing and to those places where he knew his daughters might turn up. The answer seemed to me easy enough. Those were the only night places he knew the names of. Those were the names he had heard dropped so often by his daughters. And he imagined no doubt that it made him seem much less aged and much more sophisticated in the eyes of his youngish friends to be able to direct them to new places of amusement. I feel sure not only that this idea had occurred to my sisters but that they took a kind of perverse pride in having provided him with the very information that would permit him to make such a fool of himself.

But it was the accounts given me of Father's last night on the town that came back to me most vividly during the night before I set out for Memphis. It was an occasion when both sisters were present and when young Howard Mercer was present too—probably as the paid escort of one of them. At any rate, Betsy and Jo were there with their escorts when Father arrived at the Red Lantern. He arrived as usual with a party of people whom his two daughters had not seen before. (Always it was a totally different party.) Upon entering, he and his party advanced at once in the direction of the table which Betsy and Josephine occupied. As he drew near them, the two women looked at each other with wonder and excitement in their eyes. (This detail, from Howard of course, and passed on to me by Alex.) I am not sure, and I don't suppose *they* were sure, whether they more dreaded the confrontation that now seemed inevitable or anticipated it with a certain ecstasy. In any case, as he moved toward them, his two daughters simultaneously recognized something strange and astonishing in Father's appearance. He was *not* wearing his horn-rimmed spectacles. Either he had been fitted with contact lenses or his daughters were going to have a reprieve. In view of his cataract operation three years earlier, the former seemed extremely unlikely. And the latter of course evolved to be the case. Without his spectacles he could scarcely see his hand before his face. Finally, before he and his friends were seated at a table some ten feet away from his daughters, he briefly turned his face in their direction and gazed at them without a flicker of recognition. The evening proceeded during the next hour without notable event. The old man was even able to "attempt to dance" and did quite as well as he had on previous nights. From where my sisters were sitting they could manage to see now and then that Father's hand was resting on the hand of the "youngish woman" seated beside him at the table. But at last, after just returning from the dance floor with Father, this woman excused herself and made her way to the women's rest room. Then, after a few minutes, Father himself rose, and after seeming to ask direction from another man at his table, began moving cautiously toward the two rest-room doors. No doubt he had purposely waited till this time when there was no music playing and when there was therefore no one else on the dance floor. He succeeded well enough—without his spectacles, that is—until he reached the two doors that were side by side in the far wall of the room, doors marked "Ladies" and "Gents." Betsy and Josephine were watching with certain admiration for how very well he seemed to be managing. And each was thinking, as they would later write me, how characteristic this seemed of Father. Josephine remarked in her letter to me that Father had always had a way of involving himself in difficult situations but of managing always to extricate himself by some drastic maneuver and to end by finding himself in a better position than before. Her point was, moreover, that this was not to be the case on the present occasion.

The two sisters watched with considerable admiration and, I suppose, even satisfaction, until to their utter consternation they realized—again simultaneously—that Father had mistaken the wrong door for his intended door. He presently disappeared beyond the wrong door. He remained there out of view for only a few seconds. And when he reappeared he made no move toward the right door. Instead, he headed out with an uncertain air and movement for his chair at the table he had left. By now the music was playing again, and he weaved like a drunken man between the dance couples, finally not moving at all in the direction of his own table. His cheeks were noticeably red—even from a distance—and my sisters speculated that he may have received a slap on his face—or possibly more than one—while inside the ladies' room.

Presently one of the men at his table observed him staggering about on the dance floor, and doubtless thinking this the result of too much drink, this man went forward to assist him. Perhaps he and the other members of the party had not witnessed the mistake Father had made, because when he was seated again and had spoken one sentence the whole table of people burst into unrestrained laughter. And Father, after seeming to gaze blankly about for a time, lowered his head to the surface of the table and rested it there. When after a time his woman companion did not return, one of the other women got up and went hastily to the rest room. There was some hurried coming and going there for several minutes—by waitresses and other women customers. And then after a while the manager of the Red Lantern, a large man with a black moustache and a black bow tie, approached Father's table and placed a hand heavily on his shoulder. Immediately afterward the man who had assisted Father from the dance floor helped him to his feet. Then the two of them, without waiting for the return of Father's companion, took their hats and coats and made their exit through a side door which the manager showed them to.

I think my two sisters remained a little longer but not long enough to ascertain whether Father's friend in the rest room would ever return to the table. In Josephine's letter she said: "You see how ridiculously far matters have gone. I don't know how Father will emerge from all this, but you know what he's like. He has great resilience. There's nothing to be done except to keep a watchful eye upon the dear old fellow. Maybe last night will be the end of his foolishness. Who can say? Anyway, one can only try to keep one's sense of humor and see the funny side of his adventures. After all, he is still our father. We belong to him, and he belongs to us."

7

W H E N   I   G O T the calls about Mrs. Stockwell and poor
old Father, I was already suffering from trying to live alone
without Holly and already thinking about how it would be
to grow old in such isolation as I now had come to. Holly
had been gone only a week, and already there had ceased to
be even random calls for her on our telephone. I think that
ordinarily I might have entered into my sisters' concerns
about Father with a certain glee, though I would not certainly
have considered going down to participate in whatever interference they were going to undertake against the betrothed
pair. But I would vaguely have felt that Betsy and Jo were
"within their rights" and were acting within the line of duty
in preventing the old geezer—as I might under those circumstances have phrased it—in preventing him, that is, from
making a final and absolute fool of himself. And I would not
have questioned their wisdom in thinking of their own interests in terms of Father's will. Why on earth, I might have
found myself asking, should the undistinguished Mrs. Clara

Stockwell become the sole heir to the tidy fortune Father had amassed in his very lucrative law practice of the past thirty years? There was no longer any land in the family of course—and no grandchildren to be thought of—but there were other, personal features of the estate to be considered. There were sets of flat silver, two of very great age and one with gold-washed coffee spoons, sets of silver tea service and innumerable candelabra, almost all of which had belonged to the grandmother in Nashville or the great-grandmother in Richmond. There was furniture dating from even further back, including the two massive wardrobes, "made on the place" by one of the slaves up at Thornton and hauled about by Father wherever we lived, to hold his most valued clothing. (Taken even to Vanderbilt, perhaps, even when he was an undergraduate.) And then there was the great bulk of big mahogany Victorian pieces, the mirrored sideboard, the bedroom suites, the breakfront, all of it acquired by the grandmother in Nashville and the great-grandmother in Richmond. Thinking of those possessions, which we had been taught by our grandmother to admire and revere in our childhood (though I myself had never cared for any of it at all), I might along with my sisters have asked: Why should the undistinguished Mrs. Clara Stockwell, as surviving widow, be heiress finally to all that, she who would no doubt set such store by those possessions as to incline her to marrying the old octogenarian Mr. George Carver?

But the fact was, my own present circumstances had much more influence upon me that twilight hour in Manhattan than any memory of those things which I had never really valued. After I had finally turned up the light in my apartment that Sunday, the place seemed somehow emptier to me than it had during the long day I had just got through. The ugly arbitrary furnishings that Holly and I had bought secondhand out of other people's apartments seemed to have nothing more to do with me or my life than did those family antiques in Memphis. Holly and I had often thought those pieces we had assembled rather comical-looking, even when we had bought them. Our friends were sometimes incredulous when we showed them an oak chair or a table or bedstead we had picked up for a song at some private sale—incredulous, that is, that we had actually bought it at any price whatsoever and brought it home to live with. It was not the kind of furniture either of us had grown up with, but we felt that the presence of such plain objects in our rooms was proof of our not having succumbed to the sentimental aesthetics of domesticity. Even the pictures on our walls seemed to me, this night of my life, devoid of any warmth or vitality. Holly and I had selected most of those pictures together, and they represented our common intellectual interests. There was the cruel profile of a Doge of Venice. There were two versions of the mathematically accurate representation of a Renaissance battle, with the knights' steeds looking like wooden ponies on a carrousel. And there were any number of contemporary abstractions which even we were never sure we had hung right side up. There was nothing in the place I had affection for or felt in any way close to. And yet here I was settled in with all this junk for the rest of my life. I envied Holly off in some other apartment with junk that someone else had picked up for a song at just such sales as we had gone to. I felt despair when trying to think of how to get rid of it all. I wouldn't have any idea of how to begin the process or any notion of what I would replace it with. I would just have to walk off and leave it. That seemed the likeliest solution. It was just because Holly had felt I would never be able to settle myself comfortably again in another apartment that she had insisted upon *her* moving out, instead of my doing so. And certainly

I knew I'd never be able to persuade any other vaguely youthful woman to move into an apartment with this stuff. It occurred to me that with regard to furniture mine was quite the reverse of Father's situation.

But it did make my thoughts return to Father. I was aware that it would be another hour before the actual time for putting on lights in Memphis houses. Yet I could visualize him plainly moving about in the semi-darkness, as I had just done, and putting on lights everywhere. He was a very tall, straight old man, and I could see him bending stiffly to turn the little buttons on the table lamps. I felt almost like bursting into tears. He appeared such a forlorn figure there, utterly pathetic and altogether vulnerable in his ignorance of how his two daughters at that very moment were preparing to proceed against him and were on the telephone with me, inviting me to conspire with them against him. It didn't matter that the furniture he found all about him consisted of Mother's claw-footed Federal settees and window seats and Victorian mahogany pieces and walnut desks and breakfronts and rosewood beds, as well as charming old gilt-framed family portraits. Father's furniture was, more than our own furniture even, the kind of stuff Holly and I hoped never to live with again. (Though my family always thought of it as being a rare collection of Southern antiques, it was probably not very different from the furniture one would have found in the house of a rich old Jewish family in Cleveland.) At any rate, I tried to see Father's surroundings now through his own eyes. And I was certain he was no less lonely than I for living surrounded by objects for which he had reverence and even genuine affection. His loneliness was perhaps even more profound just because of them. Identifying thus with Father, I resolved suddenly then to go back to the telephone and make reservations for my flight tomorrow morning. (It somehow always gave me extra energy to pretend I was really like my father. It did so even when I was a boy.) I resolved, moreover, to telephone him at once that I would be arriving. I would also telephone my sisters, of course, so that they would not feel that I had been in any sense disingenuous or underhanded. And of course I would be sure then that one of the two sisters would be at the airport to meet me.

I MADE THE reservations with no difficulty. I would leave La Guardia at 8 a.m. and arrive in Memphis at 10:15 a.m. My only difficulty lay in actually reaching my father or my sisters on the telephone. There was no answer at any of their numbers. By this time they would all be on their way to have supper with Mrs. Stockwell in the Red Room at the Country Club. My sisters both must have left for the Club immediately after calling me. Father would no doubt be driving his convertible (a car nearly fifteen years old but kept in perfect condition—both body and motor). He would be driving out Poplar Pike toward Germantown, on his way to fetch Mrs. Stockwell. I dialed his number, and when I heard the buzz of the phone, ringing away in that empty house, I reminded myself that Horace and Maud, the current imports from Thornton, would not be on the place. Like all old-fashioned Memphis servants, no matter how faithful, they still took Thursday and Sunday nights off. Even Mother's death, as I knew for a fact, had not changed that. It occurred to me that I could have Father paged, later on, at the Club. I was now that eager to have him know that I was coming. Yet I knew that it was going to be a trying evening for them all, with my sisters confronting Mrs. Stockwell for the first time, and that I ought not to add to the tensions. Instead, I sent each of them a telegram at home, giving my flight num-

ber and my arrival time. The messages would no doubt be
delivered in the morning after I was already airborne. But one
of my sisters would certainly manage to meet the plane.

After I had been in bed a long while and had lain there
going over in my head those letters about Father's nightlife, it
occurred to me suddenly that instead of dispatching those
telegrams I ought simply to have telephoned Alex Mercer.
He would, if I called him now even, get in touch with Father
for me, and one way or another I was bound to need his
services after I arrived. I climbed out of bed, went back to
the loggia, and dialed Alex's telephone number in Memphis.
He answered at once. He assured me that he would be there
to meet me tomorrow and that he would manage to alert
Father to the fact that I was on my way. He would do so
before he went to bed. He didn't want my telegram to Mr.
George, as he said, to come as too much of a shock. All Alex
said and the mere sound of his voice, for that matter, were
reassuring to me. After talking to him I was able to sleep.

ON THE PLANE to Memphis that Monday morning I
dozed frequently, trying to make up for the wakeful periods
of the night before. During those frequent naps I did not
dream, and I woke after each nap clearheaded about where
I was and what my mission in Memphis was. I thought primarily of what lay ahead for me—or of what I thought lay
ahead—and it seemed to me that I did certainly have a mission to perform. I felt all the enthusiasm of an old-time evan-
gelist. During the hours since I had got my sisters' calls for
assistance in the vendettas which I imagined them to be preparing, I myself had descended into an area of memory that I
had long since learned to repress. I had relived all the wrongs
done me by my father, even those he had unwittingly done
and those he had done merely in order to enable himself to go

ahead with his own life. I knew that he could not possibly have been aware, when he faced the very real necessity for himself of removing himself from the unhappy scene in which Lewis Shackleford had betrayed him, could not have imagined then that for the little thirteen-year-old boy in his household the removal would constitute a trauma he would in some way never recover from. His experiences and mine were so utterly different at that moment in life! How *could* the man have known the difference since the whole action of the little boy's drama existed not within the house or within the confines of that little estate off Franklin Pike but rather at the young people's events of the annual horse show and at Miss Cecilia Wright's dancing classes. How could he understand the disappointment and shock the boy would experience at having the important transition of puberty and adolescence so abruptly interrupted? How could he have known, being the sort of man he was or not being, rather, a more intellectual and perceptive man than he was, not a man, that is, who could look back at his own adolescence and by so doing comprehend what his son was experiencing? The fault I found with myself that night and next morning, in my present mature view of human nature, my fault was that I had at that tender age of thirteen, and always afterward in dealing with my father, repressed my feelings about my father's conduct. I had found no voice within me to protest. (But I knew I ought to have found the voice and having spoken out at the proper time ought by now to have forgotten all seeming injustice. Probably his own conflicts with *his* father he *had* protested and forgotten. That was the essence of maturity in a son.) And yet had I not, after all, been taught by my mother from some early age which I could not even remember and instructed by her even at the time of Father's betrayal and our removal that it was my civilized and Christian obligation to repress my own feelings of rebellion? It was Mother who taught us all that obligation. Was it not because of her that I had repressed any protest I might have made? It was my mother and my grandmother and all our heritage that taught us we must not rebel against that supreme authority, Mr. George Carver. And it was my fault that I had accepted their teaching so very literally. Only my brother Georgie did not do so. Georgie had paid it lip service and had gone his own way. . . . And so I had been at fault like my father and my mother through human error and through failure of understanding. I ought as a young man to have asserted my feelings of resentment, to have protested what I thought was parental injustice, and then to have forgotten the whole business. But now, since I had not, it was the part of maturity to forget those old conflicts.

I don't know that I could have reached this conclusion so readily at this time had I not felt my own loneliness, in Holly's absence. But at any rate my conviction was no less firm and profound. I knew that after first protecting Father from my sisters, I must then convert the two middle-aged women to my own views on forgetting wrongs done them by their parents. "Forget, forget," I kept insisting silently, as if further to convince myself before confronting Betsy and Josephine. I resolved that my sisters must be made to accept my doctrine of forgetting. It was too late to forgive, of course. And vengeance was not the alternative. I would say to Betsy and Josephine that forgiveness and vengeance must be the Lord's prerogative. Our prerogative was to forget the wrongs done us in our youth and childhood, in order to know ourselves truly grown up. My new insight seemed a great light casting its rays everywhere. My zeal was such that I all but forgot I still did not know how Betsy and Josephine were going to proceed or what actions would be required of me in defense of my old father. And that defense must be achieved before I could even begin my efforts to enlighten and convert the ostensible victimizers themselves.

FATHER'S PRESENCE at the airport when I arrived, soon after ten o'clock, came as a complete and singular surprise to me. It was so unexpected that it made me begin preparing myself at once for greater surprises still. Even before I descended the steps from the airplane I was convinced there had been new developments since the telephone calls last night. What struck me first was the very unlikeliness of Father's actually climbing into his car and riding to the airport. He was a man who never ran any such domestic errands or, for that matter, had never done any domestic chore whatsoever unless it was a part of his attentions to Mother, as an invalid. I never in my years at home saw him do so much as poke the fire or fetch the evening paper from the front porch —certainly not if a servant was on the place. I doubt that he had ever before this day met a member of the family at an incoming train or airplane. During the previous twenty-odd years of my homecomings it had always been one of "the girls" who was dispatched to meet me.

He wasn't waiting for me in the airport lobby. It was not so simple as that. As soon as we began our descent from the air I spotted him down there on the very edge of the runway, a tiny figure in a navy-blue topcoat and a gray homburg hat. He was gesturing with raised arms and gloved hands almost as if directing the descent and landing of the big plane. Seeing him down there in that dangerous zone I could scarcely believe my eyes. I told myself that I must be mistaken, that the figure was too tiny for me to be certain of it. It must be one of the airport staff, got up to look like Father. Yet the closer we drew in of course, the more certain I became. Even with my first glimpse, however, when he appeared no larger than a matchstick, there could have been no mistaking. The figure was altogether and profoundly familiar—and became more so with the man's every gesture—for me to be mistaken even at so great a distance.

I understood from the first moments that since the telephone calls last night there had been some momentous development. In retrospect, it seems to me that looking out my window on the plane I understood perfectly—though of course I did not—what Father would actually tell me a few minutes later: that he and Mrs. Stockwell were going to be married at noon today, that she was already waiting for him at the Presbyterian church near her house, and that I was to be present as best man. I didn't actually know this, of course, while I was still on the plane or while I stood in the plane hatchway after the flight of steps had been lowered and we were beginning to deplane. And during the minutes when we were landing and when we went rolling past the spot where Father stood and when we presently returned to stop at our arrival gate, I had no real knowledge of what Father's presence signified. And all the while, I was actually observing, without its really registering with me till later, that members of the airport staff and crew were collected at Gate Number Eight, where we were supposed to deplane. And I had seen, without being aware of its significance, that now and again one of them would dart out toward Father and then turn back. Meanwhile, at the gate entrance some of the same uniformed men were conferring with another familiar-looking person. And this person was sometimes shaking a finger at them and sometimes a fist. It gradually dawned upon me of course that this figure was none other than that of Alex Mercer.

What had struck me most forcibly at first was the very unlikelihood of Father's having climbed into his old convertible that morning and driven out to the airport and waited for a plane to come in. (It would turn out that Alex had brought him in his car.) Though always in the past it had been one or both of "the girls" who were designated to meet my incoming plane, here today was Father waving his arms rather wildly as I stepped into his view at the top of the flight of steps. I realized then that all along he had been waving at me, not trying to direct the plane's landing. From Father these antics seemed very strange indeed and yet in a sense they were very like him. He had felt sure beyond any shadow of a doubt that I would be looking at him through my little two square feet of window on the plane. He had *willed* that I should be. Moreover, he would, I thought to myself, have *known* beforehand that this was the very plane I would be aboard. He had known it regardless of any announcements over the amplifiers inside the terminal building, altogether in control of things—as in the old days. At one point I observed that the plane arriving at the next gate had pulled in very close and that an enclosed accordion passageway had been stretched out to unload the passengers. It occurred to me, quite irrationally, that it was by order of Father that we had been denied that convenience. He had arranged matters so that I would receive just the view and impression of him that I did, and it occurred to me for the first time that he had been doing that all my life—posing, that is, for my benefit and for that of the whole family. He had never faked but had always made sure that he gave the true impression of what his role was. His accurate posing and even his manner of dressing had been—that morning on the Bruce School playground as well as this morning at the airport—his most direct means of communicating his aspirations and his actual vision of how things were with him. It was, as he doubtless intended it to be, rather perplexing. In my mind it was hard to identify that vigorous and vital-seeming figure in the gray homburg and the navy

topcoat with the ineffectual old fellow whom the widow-
ladies had forced to come round to their supper parties or
with that old man whom the youngish women had humiliated
in the Memphis night spots. He seemed not at all the old man
my sisters had been describing to me in their letters. Rather,
he was the father I remembered from my early boyhood, a
commanding figure very much in charge of events. He was
the father figure I had always carried in my mind somewhat
apart from the other images I had had of him over the years.
     And suddenly I dreaded him—dreaded him as I used to
dread him sometimes when coming home from Army camp,
on leave. My impulse when I stood in the plane's exit hatch
was to duck back inside, to let him feel if only momentarily
that he had been wrong in his certainty that I would be
watching him through the window. I remained standing there
at the top of the steps even after deplaning passengers ahead
of me had descended and left the steps clear. It was then that
I saw him just as he perhaps wished me to see him or perhaps
as I needed for my own purposes to see him. He appeared as
he had appeared to me when I was a very small boy in Nashville, a person of great power and stature. I saw a flash image
of him on horseback, dressed as master of hounds and holding
the horn to his lips. I saw the man of iron will and courage
and perfect skill and limitless intelligence that I had believed
in as a small boy almost without knowing what it was I
believed.
     This impression lasted a few seconds only. But those were
important seconds and would have considerable effect on my
feelings about Father during the rest of the day. I had had the
kind of flash that one allegedly has in the moment before
death, a view of one's whole life—only my view was not of
my own but of Father's whole experience of life. The clothes
he was dressed in that morning seemed during those seconds
a kind of statement of what his entire life had amounted to

and of how he accepted it. There was no compromise in his attire. It expressed rather a positive acceptance of circumstances—of fate. If Alex Mercer's father was right in saying that the best human being is that one who adjusts best to the changing circumstances of life, then my father was superb. It was difficult to think of the old man in the navy topcoat, tailored as it obviously was by a black tailor on Beale Street, and wearing the tweed suit underneath from the same tailor, it was difficult, that is, to think of him as the same man who appeared in a morning suit on the Bruce School playground more than thirty years before. He was the same man, of course, but over the years he had managed to take on the coloration of his immediate environment, as his four Nashville children and his Nashville wife had never managed to do.

As I came down the steps from the plane it seemed to me —or perhaps it only seems so in retrospect—that there was something in his attire to suggest every phase or period of his life and all of it integrated with or subjugated to what would seem—at least to a passing observer—his pure Memphis style. His hat was what one identified first, of course, if one began to dissect. The hat was neither Nashville nor Memphis but reached further back to his own boyhood really and reflected something of his own father and grandfather. For this father of mine was not of course, himself, a Nashville-born man. As I have already explained, his father and grandfather had been country lawyers and landowners, farming sizable cotton farms in the fertile land along the Forked Deer River, farms altogether surrounding the old town of Thornton, which is in upper West Tennessee and not very far from Reelfoot Lake. Father himself was of course born up there in an old hip-roofed brick house. (It was the house in which I myself was also born. Father had insisted upon Mother's coming out from Nashville to Thornton for each lying-in, so that all of his children would be born in that house. Or perhaps Grandfather had insisted upon it.) It was a house on the largest of the family farms, a farm which came up to the very town limits of Thornton. It seems that when a local gentleman was on the courthouse square of Thornton or when he was walking his own land in that part of the world, a hat was a very important item of apparel. Father's father and his grandfather always ordered their hats from a manufacturer in St. Louis, and Father did so too, wherever he might be living. Even I can remember, as a small child, seeing my father and my paternal grandfather and great-grandfather, for that matter, in their hats walking the farm roads on the Town Farm, as we called it, or crossing the wide, wooden blocks in the streets on the courthouse square. In their law practice and even in their wide-ranging farm dealings (they also owned cotton farms in western Kentucky as well as in southern Illinois and southeastern Missouri) there were various occasions in the year when it was necessary for them to visit St. Louis and Chicago. Whether those visits related to their law practice or to their landowning I don't know. Anyhow, it was always in St. Louis that they bought their hats and in Chicago whatsoever sporting equipment they owned. They shopped there in person for those articles or they ordered them through the mail from "houses" where they were known. They spoke of St. Louis as their "hat place," and Father continued to do so always. I am sure it was in a St. Louis hat that he met me that near noonday when I arrived at the Memphis airport. On the other hand, his shoes would always be Nashville shoes. I suppose he began buying them there when he first went as a student to Vanderbilt. Or perhaps it was later, after he met Mother and entered law school. Or he may not have discovered Nashville shoes until after he and Mother were married and he came for a time to live with her family in the great stone mansion on West End Avenue. One of my early recollections is of seeing row upon row of his shoes on the shelves of his gigantic walnut wardrobe, all of them perfectly polished and in perfect repair, and every pair of the lot kept in their perfect shape by heavy wooden shoe trees. And I remember just as well his *other* wardrobe, made of cherry wood and containing always whatsoever suits, topcoats, or sports jackets were in season. (Those out of season were stored away, by Mother and Harriet or Tommie May or Maud, in cedar wardrobes up in the attic.) My father and mother very early in their marriage bought the small estate on Franklin Pike which just by chance bordered the much larger estate of Lewis Shackleford. But when my paternal grandfather was dying he ordered them to Thornton, where Father briefly assumed duties in the law firm and in the business of operating the farms. Grandfather was dead within less than a year, and it was then that one Lewis Shackleford, former water boy for the Vanderbilt football squad and now Nashville's greatest financier, though barely thirty, urged Father to return to Nashville as his chief legal counsel and adviser. I remember almost nothing of that year which our family spent in Thornton. I was not yet four years old when Grandfather bade Father come home. But I do remember seeing the wardrobes being taken from the old house when we went back to Nashville. It may have been the first removal of Father's wardrobes. (For I am not, after all, sure he took the wardrobes to Vanderbilt when he went there as a student. It would seem unlikely for anyone other than Father, and yet he had cared such a great deal for clothes even as a child, and so it would not have been out of character.) And it is the wardrobes more than anything else I remember about all the physical removals in subsequent years. The wardrobes were always the last pieces of furniture to be loaded and the first to be unloaded, always with Father watching over them to make sure the movers didn't steal any of the precious possessions inside. When finally they were put aboard the van he stood close by to oversee the heaving-to, the shifting and shoving, making sure to the last that they were handled with the greatest care. I remember his more than once telling the moving men, who showed interest in the matter, that the wardrobes had been made "on the place" in his great-grandfather's time. By "on the place" he of course meant on the Town Farm at Thornton.

WHEN AT LAST I had descended the plane steps and came up to where my father was standing alone on the expanse of asphalt and where the airport staffers had finally abandoned him, now that danger was past, it was as though someone had thrown open the double doors to one of those wardrobes of his and, figuratively speaking, I was inhaling the familiar aroma of his whole life and being. Only it wasn't like an aroma exactly. For one moment it seemed I was about to be suffocated. For one moment it was as if I had never left Memphis. It was as if my two sisters had not made possible my escape that winter morning long ago, as though they had not come forward with warm reassurances and with loans of money and had not seen me on that plane to New York at an hour when Father was still asleep in his bed.

As Father and I finally stood face to face, all the other deplaning passengers were dashing past us toward the terminal building. Alex Mercer, no longer engaged by the depot people, was waiting patiently at Gate Number Eight, wearing his big, belted all-weather overcoat and his knit cap with ear-flaps. And now Father seized my right hand between his own gray-kid-gloved hands. I remember glancing down and observing that even the black stitches in those gray kid gloves had an elegance about them that sent a wave of nostalgia through me. But he exerted such pressure on my hand that I had perforce to look up at him and gaze nowhere but into

his radiant blue eyes. The look in his eyes, the very smile on
his thin lips told me better than any words could have done
how overjoyed he was that I was there to support him. His
pressure on my hand was overpowering to any reservations I
might have tried to summon up about him at that moment.
The very way he swayed his broad shoulders from left to
right and back again as he smiled at me and pressed my hand
made him seem irresistible. I could recall his greeting other
people this way. In particular I momentarily recalled the first
time he ever shook Alex Mercer's hand. But he had never
before in my life given me such a greeting. He seemed not like
the old man described in Betsy's and Josephine's or in Alex's
letters but a much younger and more vigorous man than I
had seen the last time I was home.

He began at once by telling me that he was going to be
married at high noon, that very day, and that he wanted me
to "stand up" with him. I said nothing but assented with a
smile and a slow nod of my head. Then he asked if the bag
I carried with my left hand was my only luggage. When I
indicated that it was, he rejoiced anew. And I grasped at once
that my not having other luggage meant to him that we would
not be delayed by waiting at the baggage-claim window. As
he and I moved toward the gate where Alex waited, I noticed Father glancing about almost furtively. And his every
step seemed a little more hurried than the one before. Even
then I began suspecting that he feared my two sisters might
be in hiding somewhere, ready to interrupt his progress and
pounce upon him at any moment. He explained to me as we
walked that he and Mrs. Stockwell had already obtained their
marriage license and that it had been arranged for the Presbyterian parson to meet them at the church. These plans had of
course been made before he knew that I would be present for
the ceremony. My own arrival today, he assured me in the
gentlest voice, was one of those "great and wonderful coinci-

dences that make the difference between success and glorious success."

"Such coincidences," he declared, almost chattering away now and still peering rather nervously in first one and then another direction, "such coincidences are sometimes what one must depend upon to make life seem worth living." He told me that Mrs. Stockwell would be no less elated than he by my presence but explained that he had not been able to let her know of my coming. Alex had reached *him* on the telephone with this news scarcely two hours ago, and the bride-to-be in the rush of all she had to do was not answering her telephone this morning. But she and a woman friend would join them in the parson's office at a quarter till twelve. She of course would be expecting Alex Mercer to perform as best man. But now we were at the gate, and Alex himself was greeting me with a warmth no less than that Father had shown. One would have thought that it was as a favor to him, Alex Mercer, that I had come. As we three moved through the vast new airport at a decidedly rapid pace the idea of his being an eighty-one-year-old man seemed unthinkable. It was he who set the pace for the two younger men on either side of him, and of course he was without his cane today. One could only assume that on this day at least—or at this hour of this day—all his ailments, indeed all evidence of advanced age, were in total remission. His gait was livelier than that of either of the younger men. He was certainly better dressed and better groomed. Even his broad-brimmed felt hat had a rakish quality about it, turned up in the back and perched at a slight angle over his left eye. Neither Alex's knit cap nor my little, narrow-brimmed Tyrolean number could compare for style.

Yet as we passed through the main lobby and down the escalator to the glass doors leading to the parking lot, he continued to cast suspicious glances around every pillar, into every corner, down every passageway. It was only when we had crossed the wide parking lot and he and I were safely ensconced in the back seat of Alex Mercer's old Chevy that Father relaxed and began telling me again with a bright look in his blue eyes how glad he was to have me there. It was Alex who had insisted that Father and I sit together in the rear seat of the car, but Father offered no resistance and soon after we had settled ourselves in I felt him slip his arm through mine. It remained there for the duration of our ride to the Presbyterian church. How, I asked myself, could one resist such paternal attentions and advances? I tried to resist, though, if only because I felt a certain guilt for my own weakness in his presence. I was thinking also of my two sisters, wondering if by any chance they might really have been concealed somewhat in the airport—behind some pillar, in some corner, behind some magazine rack or some food-vending machine— and if they really might yet manage to interfere with the nuptial plans of the old couple.

But at last I relaxed in the back seat of Alex's Chevy. I sat with Father's arm locked in mine and now I was completely under his spell. I felt no guilt whatsoever about recalling my old resentments while simultaneously responding to his warm clasp. The theme that kept returning to me all the while, like a phrase from some musical composition that I had recently purchased a recording of but had not learned entirely and was impatient to get home to my apartment and play again, was my recently articulated theme of forgetfulness. It transcended all my many other feelings toward Father. The idea of forgetting all that I had ever held against him was like forgetting the cruelties of fate itself. And I took no credit for the willed act of forgetting. It was impossible to look upon the man's radiant face and not forget real or imagined injuries he had done me. At any rate, at this moment I went over again the profound generalization and truth that had dawned upon me earlier. Forgetting the injustices and seeming injustices which one suffered from one's parents during childhood and youth must be the major part of any maturing process. I kept repeating this to myself, as though it were a lesson I would at some future time be accountable for. A certain oblivion was what we must undergo in order to become adults and live peacefully with ourselves. Suddenly my sisters seemed no longer a mystery to me. I understood much of their past conduct as never before. They were still, while actually in their mid-fifties, two little teenaged girls dressed up and playing roles. It was their way of not facing or accepting the facts of their adult life. They could not forget the old injuries. They wished to keep them alive. They were frozen forever in their roles as injured adolescents.

IT WAS ONLY just as I felt I had attained this wonderful kind of epiphany that I saw we were turning into the driveway that made a half circle in front of the portico of the Presbyterian church. I congratulated myself that now there could be no interference and promised myself that immediately after the ceremony I would go to my sisters and make what I had done right with them. And then I observed the young minister standing on the church steps, wearing a sad, questioning smile on his lips. In his hand I saw a small pale blue envelope, looking ominously like a piece of ladies' stationery. There had been almost no talk in the car. All three of us had each been holding his breath, so to speak. Father cleared his throat and said: "Clara's not here. She's not here." He spoke through his teeth, barely parting his thin lips, which were drawn very tight.

"Maybe she's been delayed," Alex suggested hopefully from the front seat, though I think we all knew instantly that she was not coming.

"We'll see, we'll see," Father said under his breath, still speaking through his teeth. He began rolling down the window beside him. Before the minister could reach forward and take the door handle to open the door, Father had shot his hand out the car window and fairly snatched the blue envelope from the relaxed and unsuspecting hand that held it. "She isn't here?" he asked, looking into the young minister's worried brown eyes. Father simultaneously removed his hat from his head, as a sign of respect for the cloth—so I understood it—and passed it to me to hold for him. As he began opening the envelope he glanced up at the minister again. "And she isn't coming, is she?" he said tentatively, as if hoping to be contradicted. Then he read the note to himself, his lips moving ever so slightly.

The fair-skinned, brown-eyed, balding young minister was silent for a moment. Finally he said: "I think she's not." And then after another moment's silence he said to Father: "But won't you come inside? It might help to talk some."

Father looked up from the one-page note. Then he looked down again and turned the sheet over to make certain there was nothing on the other side. Without raising his eyes again he said: "No, I think it wouldn't help." Presently, still not raising his eyes, he passed the note on to me and at the same time took back his hat and restored it to his head.

Mrs. Clara Stockwell had left early that morning on a "motor trip to California," traveling in the company of a woman friend. She would be gone for three months but she did not give her precise destination. She knew, she said in the note, it was a cruel and cowardly thing she was doing. But "events had conspired" to show her there could be no happiness in a marriage between the two of them. He had his children to think of, she said. When I had read through the note, I heard Father saying: "I could wait the three months except that at my age it might seem right long." I realized only then that despite his having bent forward to take the letter from the parson and despite the removal of his hat, his left arm was still hooked through my arm. He began extracting it now and looked at me rather deprecatingly, as if to acknowledge it had been a rather foolish gesture to have put it there to begin with. With the note still in his hand, neither crushed nor torn up, he sat up very straight on the car seat, his hat squarely on his head. Meanwhile, Alex was leaning forward with his forehead resting on the steering wheel, and the young minister was looking earnestly through the window glass, which Father had rolled up again. "We had better be on our way," Father said presently. "I want to get home and see what else the girls have prepared for me." I had not expected him to say anything like that and felt a kind of shock go through me, as though I had touched an exposed electric wire. But he wore a cold, bland smile on his lips when he said it. And it was the only expression he gave to any suspicion that Betsy and Josephine had had a hand in the conspiring of events this morning or any suspicion that there might be further conspiring of events yet to come.

8

It was but a mile or so from the portico of Mrs. Stockwell's Presbyterian church to the front doorstep of Father's house. Father seemed almost to forget that Alex and I were in the car with him. From time to time he would nod his head, lift his eyebrows, compress his lips. Clearly he was in some kind of dialogue with himself, and there were no signs of senility in his behavior. I had seen him too many times before this behave in just this way when he was a younger man. How often I had seen him sitting a little apart from the rest of the family though remaining purposely in the same room with us. It meant that he was absorbed by some problem, personal or otherwise, but that he would presently manage to work it out in his head. As we rode through this east end of town he sat with his arms folded over his chest, his very blue eyes staring straight ahead. For the moment he had abandoned Alex Mercer and me, his two chief supporters in this present business. He was saying to us in effect that from this point he had to go it alone, as he had always gone everything alone the last mile, but also as always he counted on those nearest him to stand by him and not be offended by his seeming withdrawal into himself or by his continued demands upon them.

During those ten or twelve minutes between the church and the house I felt certain that either he would go to California and find Mrs. Stockwell or he would wait the three months for her to return or that he would find himself another bride, one who would at least care so much for his money and for his antique furniture and for his position in the small world of Memphis that she would not be frightened away by jealous daughters. I had every confidence that despite his age and infirmity he would in some manner or other yet prevail, and I took a final comfort in the thought that with his iron will (and in these enlightened times) there was no way my sisters could incarcerate him in a nursing home or on some cotton farm in Mississippi. There seemed no way that my sisters could do more than they had already done to stand in his way. I didn't know how it was exactly but I knew that somehow or other they had got through to Mrs. Stockwell. They would surely not repeat whatsoever it was they had done on this occasion. If they wished to do more than this, surely the price for them in pride would be too great.

But as we turned between the boxwoods at the entrance to Father's two-acre plot, I at once became aware of a large rectangular object, somehow inimical to the scene, drawn up to the house and visible at the end of the two rows of old cedars that lined the driveway. The house was set back some three hundred feet from the road, and when we had traversed half that distance I recognized the unlikely object as a commercial moving van. I was able to identify it immediately then by the name of the local storage warehouse which was writ in large red letters on the side of the van. I suspect Alex and Father recognized it at precisely the same moment I did.

Father bent forward for a better view and said: "Well, I'll
be damned! What's that all about?" As when he had spoken
earlier, his front teeth seemed on edge.

Alex Mercer asked: "Is someone moving *in* or *out*?" And
as we drew nearer I caught glimpses of three or four men
unloading onto the grass a number of cartons and crates of
various sizes as well as a variety of chairs, end tables, and
other small pieces of household furniture. And there on the
lawn were Maud in her black uniform and Horace in his
white coat, both of them lending a hand with carrying all
those things into Father's house.

"Someone's moving in," I said presently, as though wak-
ing from a dream and feeling compelled to explain it. As is
my wont regarding such moments, it seems to me now that
from the first instant I saw the van I had not a doubt in the
world who those someones moving in must be. My sisters
Betsy and Josephine were transferring all their most cherished, their really indispensable possessions from their old-
fashioned two-story houses at midtown into the spare rooms
of their father's modern one-story suburban house. They were
giving up their long-cherished independence! They were
doing so in order to prevent any future threat of a second
marriage on the part of their old father. Their giving up
their cherished independence was almost beyond belief to
me. But I understood now how great was their determination,
how committed they were to keeping Father in a lone and
single state.

When we had come to a stop outside the front door, Alex
could not be persuaded to go inside the house or even to set
one foot out of the car. I knew that he must feel that he
could not bear the sight of my sisters. And when Father and
I had alighted and I was taking my bag out of the front seat
beside him, Alex would not even turn his face in my direction to look at me. I realized that it was more than my sisters

he could not bear the sight of at this moment. He had seen enough of us all. But I kept my eyes on him as he drove down the driveway and out between the boxwoods at the entrance. He did so without casting one look backward in our direction.

When Father and I got inside the front door we were greeted most cordially by Betsy and Josephine. Each was dressed in the kind of modest, simple housedress that our mother used to wear on moving day or when she was having spring cleaning done. The dresses were full of starch and were made of some material like gingham. You could tell from the obvious creases that they were spanking new, that they had been bought for the occasion. One could tell from the dresses more than from anything else that Betsy and Josephine were beginning a new life. One perceived in their manner as well as in their attire that they were now on duty! Even between their greetings to us they were busily giving orders to the servants and to the moving men about where their possessions should "go." But they took time out to give big kisses to Father and me. Father smiled at them in much the same way he had smiled at the Presbyterian minister a few minutes earlier, except that he did not look directly at Betsy or at Josephine. Even as he spoke, he kept his eyes trained on some distant corner of the front hall. Presently, still not looking at them, he said: "Welcome home, girls." Then he went off down the passage to his own bedroom.

When he was out of earshot, Betsy and Josephine said in one voice, full of everyday friendliness and familial love: "We've come home to roost, Phil."

"Yes, I see you have," said I.

"Maud's made the daybed for you in Father's study," Josephine said to me.

But I didn't take my bag back to the study, even. I couldn't bear to spend the one night in that house with them. I couldn't bear to think of the unreal conversations that would take place there that night and in all the future. Fortunately when I telephoned the airport to make reservations I was able to get a five o'clock plane back to La Guardia.

9

I HAD BELIEVED, when I got back to New York, that I had witnessed the end of my sisters' vendetta against Father. During the next week I imagined I was writing the final chapter of my account of his entrapment. But in the months since I have returned something has happened that compels me to reopen my notebooks. I find that I must write a postscript of a kind that I would earlier have deemed the unlikeliest of possibilities.

Holly Kaplan, as I have indicated, returned to live with me within a few weeks after she departed for our trial separation. She was not there when I got back from Memphis, but I had a call from her a few days later and went down to her new apartment in the East Village to see her. Her apartment there, which she had sublet from a friend, was even dingier and darker than my place on 82nd Street. One entered through a kind of courtyard after ringing two bells for admission through the front vestibule. It was nighttime when I came, but there was a bright illumination from lamps that apparently stayed on all night. In the paved courtyard three small boys were enjoying a dreadful free-for-all fight when I passed through. There were two mothers—or seemingly that—wrapped in furs and seated on a small bench. They were engaged in pleasant, animated conversation and almost pointedly ignoring the boys' fight—and doing so, I felt somehow, for my benefit. I directed my gaze toward the doorway in a far corner, determined not to acknowledge the noise and activity of either the little boys or the mothers.

When Holly opened the door to her second-floor apartment, the darkness and dinginess that I at once became aware of beyond her slight figure seemed a welcome refuge from the bright lights and the noise in the courtyard. We went inside and sat down facing each other on two very hard straight chairs. I knew that I wished to have Holly back with me on 82nd Street, and she had told me on the telephone that she wished to come back if that turned out to be what I desired after our present interview. We sat talking there for an hour in the dim light of a single floor lamp. Our old serenity and calm had returned. Strange to relate, we talked for the first time in many months of our two families, indulging ourselves on a topic that had until now been taboo between the two of us for a number of years. Our talk began with Holly's shocking news that her own mother had died during the interval we had been apart and had died during the very time that I was in Memphis. Holly had been, herself, in Cleveland attending the funeral at that time. She had not telephoned me because she had felt that our concern or unconcern for our families was a tender point between us. I felt instantly that there had been some change in her feelings on the subject. Of course I told her the story of my disastrous one-day visit to Memphis. I could not perceive at once whether she was more sympathetic to Betsy and Josephine or to Father. She said she did not, herself, know.

Revenge was a useless and wicked thing, she said, but she wondered aloud how she would feel if her own father began talking now of marriage. When finally I left her to the gloom of her apartment and went out through the brightly lit courtyard, the little boys and the two mothers were still engaged with one another. There was something about this that seemed to lift my spirits. I thought this part of town and this apartment building might be a good place to live. But two days later I took a cab and went down to the East Village again and fetched Holly and her possessions to 82nd Street.

DURING THE DAYS and weeks that followed Holly and I talked of almost nothing but our two families and of the problems of looking after old people—of looking after aged parents in particular. Holly was meanwhile receiving letters about her father's discontent with the "retirement home" that he had been moved to. And my sisters began writing me about the new onset of Father's neuropathy and his senile diabetes. In both cases—mine and Holly's—we were urged to come home, if only to help cheer the patients. We neither of us considered going, but we went on talking about what was to be done for those two poor old souls, our fathers. If one could not bear to be with them, if only because of temperament, then how was one to offer protection and care? We were like a couple that finds itself bringing up children when there is no natural liking for children in either parent. I had been touched by Father's turning so affectionately to me, and yet in retrospect I could not fail to find it offensive, his embracing me there after so many years of coldness. Nevertheless, I could not stop thinking of him there in that house and under the watchful eyes of Betsy and Josephine. I kept remembering that at the doorway when I was leaving, Josephine had said to me under her breath that she and Betsy had decided to retire from the real estate business. This was a greater sacrifice actually and an even more frightening aspect of their vengeance than their moving back under the parental roof. It meant that they could devote all their time and energy to the monitoring of Father's confinement. At this realization I almost turned back into the house. But since neither sister had offered to drive me to the airport, I had ordered a cab, and the cab was already in the driveway. Without another word I went out and got into the cab. When I had closed the cab door I looked down at my hands and observed that they were shaking visibly. In the driver's rearview mirror I saw that my face had lost all its color. It was as if standing in the doorway my sister had told me under her breath that once I was gone the two of them were planning to put a blanket over Father's old head and slowly smother him to death.

HOLLY'S CLEVELAND letters told of her father's discontent. Most of all he disliked his little three-room apartment in the retirement home. He had brought a few pieces from the old house with him, including his mahogany rolltop desk, which piece he had insisted upon having with him, over everyone's protest. He complained that the other children and their spouses showed too much concern for him and visited him too often. When they had used to come to see him in his house and he had then grown tired of them, he could, and would, go and hide himself somewhere upstairs. But in the little retirement apartment there was no place to hide. He decided that after all he had brought too much furniture into the apartment and wished to give some of it to one or another of the children. But none of them would accept anything. They were all afraid of what the others

would say or think. For there had been considerable quarreling amongst them, at the time of their mother's funeral,
over the disposition of the furniture and the silver and the
china.

But now Holly began to admire those brothers and sisters
for the very quarreling they had done about their mother's
possessions during the days when she had lingered on after
the funeral. She found now that she envied their caring about
the various pieces of bric-a-brac and the heavy, old-fashioned
furniture. She wished she cared about it, too. She envied their
quarreling sometimes amongst themselves about anything at
all and envied even their quarreling sometimes with their old
father. She felt they had a real life out there in Cleveland
that she didn't have, had never had, would never have now.
When she left home fifteen years ago she had thought she
was going to New York to have some kind of high-powered
literary career. What a mistaken notion that was for a girl of
her unpretentious and fragile composition, a girl of her honest
nature. She had been brought up by a father—and a mother,
too—who taught her or tried to teach her that a woman's
chief function was to serve a man. Perhaps simply breaking
through that old false conception and merely slipping away
to New York to find a job had consumed all energy there
was in her for forging a different kind of life for herself.
And so she had settled for something less than a real literary
career. Her father had set out to teach her three sisters the
same lesson of submission which he had sought to teach her
and he had succeeded so well with them that he was now
unhappily surrounded by them and was the object of their
too strenuous attentions. He found it suffocating. If Holly
nowadays felt a longing to return and be a part of that life
and even have a part in their bickering over the bric-a-brac,
she knew that she could never really do so. But she was

teaching herself to admire and respect her old patriarch of a
father as she had not done since before her adolescence.
Moreover, she began teaching me at this point to seek a still
clearer understanding of my own father. She wished me to
do more than forget the old wrongs. She wished me to try
to see him in a light that would not require either forgetting
or forgiving. She frequently urged me to talk about him, as
she certainly had not urged me to do in years, and to try to
give her a whole picture of what his life had actually been
and to try to imagine how it must always have seemed to
him.

INSTEAD OF FORGETTING, I soon discovered that I
was now able to imagine more about Father's life than I had
in the past ever had any conception of—not of his professional
life or his business affairs, though I felt I understood more of
all that than I had previously realized, and not his family life
even, but his inner life, his inmost, profoundest feelings about
the world he was born into and in which he was destined to
pass his youth and most of his adult years. I felt I could almost
remember old conflicts that he must have had with his father
and that he had managed, like any healthy adult, to put out
of his head forever. It seemed I knew even his every aspiration
for himself from the time he was a small boy until his present
old age.

My father was born of course in that old hip-roofed
brick house on the Town Farm, at Thornton. He and his
father both had been born in that house to which my mother
had been required to repair whenever one of her children
was going to be born. His earliest recollections were of life
as lived on that four hundred acres of highly productive,
red-clay cotton land. His earliest adventures abroad were

fishing and swimming expeditions to the Forked Deer Farm, which was another of my grandfather's cotton farms. He must very early have been made aware that on the night he was born, at the very hour of his birth in the big downstairs bedroom of that two-story hip-roofed house, the bells in nearly all the churches of Thornton were rung. Guns were also fired on the courthouse lawn at that hour, as well as at various intersections of streets in the town. His mother—my grandmother—who died within an hour of his birth, must have heard those bells and heard that gunfire during the last moments of her life. They were the guns of men, black and white, who farmed and hunted the family's extensive landholdings in Thorn County. And the bells were those of black churches and white churches alike. Presumably only those poor and benighted congregations that had no belfries—the Campbellites and the Footwashing Baptists—did not signalize the new baby's arrival in the world. Otherwise, the arrival of no royal heir, or perhaps of no ducal heir, or at least of no squirearchical heir was ever celebrated with more warmth in any town or countryside. He was the first and only child of his parents' union, and his mother was past forty at the time of her confinement. Word has not come down as to whether or not the church bells tolled her passing with a unanimity equal to the ringing on the heir's arrival.

At any rate, the little baby George Carver was looked after by black mammies and maiden aunts, and when he was wheeled about the shady streets of Thornton, and led through the streets by the hand later on, he was looked upon as a little prince. Not only was his father the largest landowner in the county, his great-grandfather had settled there on a Revolutionary War grant, which somehow gave him the highest prerogative. Regardless of wealth or high station or education (all Father's forebears had allegedly been sent to

Princeton to be educated until the time of the Civil War), regardless of all that, everyone in any community prefers a born hero to a made hero. It means that he has the highest favor of the gods. He is born lucky! And that was how George Carver was regarded in Thornton. He didn't have extremely great wealth or very high style or station or a really superior education, but he had the best of everything that Thornton, Tennessee, had to offer. Everyone in Thornton felt he was born under a lucky star. There was a story about his rolling out of a second-story window when he was six months old and landing in a large basket of laundry which just happened to be deposited directly below the window. And through all his life he would himself be prouder of his good luck than of any of his attainments. Even when he had been financially ruined by Mr. Lewis Shackleford and was setting out for Memphis with his family, he counted on and believed in his good luck still. If one of his beautiful daughters had eloped with her young man that day at lunch in the old clapboard hotel at Huntingdon, I think he would have counted it as his first piece of personal bad luck in his life. And he would have felt it was something that he could not deal with, as he could *deal* with Lewis Shackleford's betrayal. But it was simply part of his nature to believe in his good luck, and it was this belief of his when he was a boy and young man that the citizens of Thornton recognized and admired in him as much as they acknowledged his good luck itself.

But beyond his satisfaction with his good luck to be born so well fixed materially and physically and mentally (he was of course valedictorian when he graduated from Thornton Academy) a kind of dissatisfaction began to manifest itself in the growing boy George Carver before he was in long trousers. It was of this that I sometimes used to hear him speaking to my friend Alex Mercer. And it is only now in middle age that I began to realize that it was something like this—in some sense and degree like this—that my father and my friend Alex actually had in common. The principal difference was that Alex had the puritanical conviction that he must not let himself act upon his dissatisfaction, must not yearn after that which was not his by birth, must not acknowledge the yearning even, whereas to my mind it seems almost a great beauty of my father's character that from his earliest years the boy George Carver yearned for an individuality and for personal attainments that could be in no way related to the accident of his birth, longed to succeed in some realm that he had not yet heard of and could not have heard of, yearned for some mysterious achievements that could not be had on the Town Farm or on the Thorn County Courthouse square, yearned, as I heard him put it to Alex Mercer, "for an otherness to everything I had been taught was mine or might be mine." He aspired to an individuality that could not be accounted for by the components of his own character and his own identity. He aspired to otherness than what he was by accident of birth in any sense of the phrase. At some point in his maturing into manhood this yearning and this longing and this aspiring became a craving. This, it will be understood, is what I came to feel, came to recognize, when called upon to interpret Father to Holly Kaplan. And forever afterward during his life, it seemed to me, this craving had always been present in him.

This, at any rate, was how, within a few days almost, I was brought to see the man I had for so many years thought of merely as selfish. It was mostly under Holly's influence that I came to a so much more interesting and enlightened view of him. If in the final analysis it was not an altogether accurate view, still it was at the time immensely gratifying to me. I found I had even to revise my old ideas of his friendship with Lewis Shackleford. As a little boy in Nashville I had seen the two men together under the most favorable and even, from my child's point of view, the most flattering circumstances. And I began now to reinterpret, in the light of this spell I was under, all that I had observed of that friendship.

10

THEY WERE SERIOUS men, my father and Mr.
Shackleford. There was never much banter to be heard between them. Nor was there ever much philosophizing, banal
or otherwise. I used to follow close behind them on my ill-
natured horse Red when we had all been riding to the hounds
in the Radnor Hills. We would be going at a leisurely pace
along one of the shady gravel lanes, which usually ran between two low stone walls. The foliage of the black gums
and maples and oaks often met overhead on those lanes, and
it seems to me that every morning somewhere on our ride
there would be an old Negro man bent down beside one of
the walls, making repairs. It was a timeless scene. I could not
imagine a past time when it had not been just so or a future
time when it would not be the same. As I rode beside and
behind the two men I could see that their clothes were
drenched with their own sweat from the hard riding they
had just done. And beads of sweat ran down their temples
and down the backs of their necks from underneath their

black cloth riding caps. They would be speaking with satisfaction of the chase and the jumps they had just made and
in general of this sport which in its present form had only
recently come into fashion in the wide valley we called the
Nashville Basin. I think to some extent fox hunting meant
different things to the two of them, but for each the other
was a significant factor in the pleasure received from his
own participation.

In Lewis Shackleford's eyes my father was a country
gentleman, heir to the old agrarian traditions of Europe
and the antebellum South, with which Lewis himself wished
to be identified. I am sure he never allowed himself to think
of Father merely as the son of a West Tennessee lawyer and
cotton farmer. I am sure that he imagined that Father exem-
plified all that he wished his neighbors and close companions
to exemplify. My father was an excellent horseman and a
natural athlete. When he turned to fox hunting it was no
wonder he should excel. But without analyzing it so, Lewis
felt and liked to feel that George Carver, my father, had
been born to the chase. Lewis remembered of course that he
had admired this George Carver first as the brilliant football
captain and irrepressible left end on the Vanderbilt squad
and he knew that as a boy fox hunting had not been an
equestrian sport for him but one practiced on foot—that is,
standing for most of the night around a fire in the woods and
listening to the voices of the hounds. Yet Lewis did not let
this knowledge stand in the way of the conception he wished
and needed to have of his friend.

Although Father knew that Lewis Shackleford was the
son of a self-made Nashville banker and businessman and
had only recently taken up the country life, he knew also
that Lewis nowadays sometimes rode to the hounds up in
New York State, at Westchester, and even in Massachusetts,
at Ipswich, and even across the water in Ireland and Scotland.

He was aware of all Lewis Shackleford's connections and of from where it was Lewis had brought home many of his notions of how to live. Yet in Father's case, Nashville was the height of his aspirations. His aspirations never went farther, I think, though they might have done so if events had turned out differently. However that may be, as the two men rode along beside each other down the Tennessee lane their mutual admiration sounded in their voices and was recognizable even to the innocent ears of a small boy. Even the boy could perceive that both were men of considerable imagination, though he could not have said this in so many words. Not then he couldn't. But in retrospect long afterward the boy, myself of course, learned to admire them for aspiring to be something more than just the businessman and his lawyer, trying to build a financial empire through the purchase and sale of municipal bonds of small Southern cities. It would later seem wonderful to me that they never talked shop when I went fox hunting or bird shooting or trout fishing with them. They talked of the biographies they were forever reading and recommending to each other—biographies of such men as Jefferson and Jackson and even Aaron Burr, popular books of the day that I of course would not today allow in my library, certainly not in my collection of rare books. Once, years later, in my father's library in Memphis, I came upon a book called *My Autobiography*, by Benito Mussolini, and on the flyleaf was inscribed: "To George Carver with great esteem—Lewis Shackleford." Only that. It was dated "Christmas 1927."

SOMETIMES ON SATURDAYS my father and Lewis would go swimming in a big public pool that had recently been opened at the village of Franklin. My mother and Mrs. Shackleford would be along too, as well as Lewis

Shackleford's old mother and even Mrs. Shackleford's mother
and even sometimes my own mother's mother. There would
also be my two sisters and my brother Georgie and myself.
The Shacklefords had no children of their own but liked to
include us, the Carver children, in such informal gatherings.
I spent many hours with them at their big neo-Georgian
mansion, perched on a hill within view of our own house,
and went with them on many expeditions like those to the
Franklin pool. My mother and Mrs. Shackleford were not
particularly congenial but they remained always on the best
of terms. In age they were at least half a generation apart,
Mrs. Shackleford being at least ten years younger than her
husband, and Lewis himself being nearly as much younger
than my father. But Mother and Mrs. Shackleford's mother,
who had known each other all their lives, now became very
close friends. On the swimming expeditions Mother and the
two older ladies—and sometimes my grandmother—would
sit on the edge of the pool, wearing very modest bathing
suits, and never getting into the water. They would chatter
at each other about old times in Nashville when all of them
were girls there. Mother was much younger than the other
three women who sat at the edge of the pool. She had very
pretty arms and legs, and underneath her dark bathing suit
her figure was still shapely. With her long hair pushed up
under her tight bathing cap, her long face looked somehow
like that of a young girl. I thought her much the most attractive girl or woman in the whole area around the swimming
pool. Now and then you would hear a peal of laughter from
her little group at the poolside and you would see one of
them—usually Mother herself—indicating with both hands
how some dress she had worn in the old days had been "cut."
Meanwhile, the youthful Mrs. Shackleford—Mary Ann we
all called her—and my two sisters would often be paddling
about together or standing in the shallow water, engaged

in their own animated conversation. And my brother Georgie would likely have abandoned all family groups and would be chasing about with newly made friends of precisely his own age. He cared nothing for any person who was so much as a year younger or a year older than himself. And this was typical of Georgie's mentality. But as for me, I would often as not be watching Father and Mr. Lewis Shackleford, watching them from some quiet backwater of the big pool. Either they would be swimming together very slowly across the pool, which was oval in shape—always talking, talking. Or they would be furiously and seemingly quite independent of each other swimming the length of the long pool, each in his own vigorous version of the crawl but each, in my view at least off in some curved recess of the pool, each aware of the other's style.

There was one occasion, when the two men had finished their exercise and I had, myself, had enough of the water, that I chose to follow them inside the men's locker room. When I came in to where they were, they had stripped off their wet suits and were seated at opposite ends of the same wooden bench with white towels thrown about their shoulders. And they were still talking, talking, talking. I remember that Lewis sat with his hands clasped about one knee, holding that knee considerably higher than the other and with his foot dangling above the cement floor. He sat there casually as if he had been fully clothed and perhaps in the boardroom of his downtown office. While they talked on, I came up even closer to them since my own clothes were in a locker just behind the bench on which they were sitting. They went on talking, unaware of their own nakedness and of my standing there before them rather impatiently. That is how I often think of them when remembering the intimacy of their friendship. Father was not yet forty-five at the time, and Lewis Shackleford, though already the head of his own in-

vestment banking house—already termed a financial empire
by unfriendly newspapers—was scarcely more than thirty-
five. Their steel-trap minds—so friendly newspapers would
have it—and their remarkable energies must certainly have
been at their peak, and their bodies were still the bodies of
young men in their prime. (My father had been called "Black"
Carver on the Vanderbilt football team, and his head never
looked blacker than when in contrast, as it was that day in
the locker room, with the full exposure of his very white
naked body.) I do not wonder that I often think of the two
men as they were that day in the Franklin pool locker room,
naked and altogether relaxed in each other's company. It was
as if, or so it would seem to me in retrospect when I was a
man older than either of them was that day, as if some naïve
painter had posed them together in his wish to represent two
opposites in human character. My father's was still the wide-
shouldered, narrow-hipped body of the left end on the football squad. There was still no suggestion of a paunch at his
midriff, and his upper arm muscles were as firm and as
smoothly rounded as ever they had been. Lewis Shackleford's
long, angular frame was not much more muscular than my
brother Georgie's early-adolescent physique. For some reason
I noticed particularly Lewis's long shin bones, his long,
straight nose, and his freckled shoulders that were a little
bit rounded and seemed almost like a girl's.

When at last the two men seemed to become aware of my
presence before them, even then they did not change their
relaxed positions or cease their talking. Father only indicated
with his left hand that I should step over the bench to gain
access to my locker. He looked at me then with those blue
eyes of his almost as if unseeingly. His blue eyes gazed ab-
stractedly at me from underneath his shock of black hair,
his hair still glistening in its wetness. And Lewis Shackleford
looked at me similarly. His brown eyes always seemed pierc-

ing because of his long nose, I think. He looked at you from under heavy dark eyebrows and from beneath an almost freakishly large forehead. I think I noticed for the first time that day how thin his blond hair had become, though I believe he had only that summer turned thirty-five, and how far the hairline had receded on his broad, high forehead.

BUT SOMETIMES I observed Lewis Shackleford and Father in circumstances and surroundings of an opposite kind—that is, not naked and talking at random about the many interests in life they shared. I saw them in their offices downtown and saw them there clothed in all their worldly paraphernalia. It was usually on a Sunday afternoon or some-times on a weeknight that I would be taken along to a special meeting of Shackleford and Company's board of directors. I would be taken along and allowed to spend the time rum-maging through Father's office and wandering through other rooms of the empty building—it being after office hours— and even sometimes wandering into the meeting room to sit silently in a straight chair against the wall. It was I who was taken along on these occasions simply because I asked to go and because Georgie did not ask. It is a certainty that at this time in our lives my father believed that he and I were tem-peramentally and intellectually very much alike. There would come a day later on, at about the time when we left Nash-ville and made our move to Memphis, that he and I would discover almost simultaneously that our only resemblance lay in our personal appearance, and even there, there was a total difference in coloring. But in those days in Nashville he was convinced that I was going to grow into the man who would be his great satisfaction as a son. I am sure, too, that he must have conveyed this idea to Lewis Shackleford. During those board meetings when I would be sitting straight against the wall I would see Father's blue eyes fixed on me for one fleeting second, and I sensed the satisfaction he took from my presence and my attention. And in another moment I would see Lewis Shackleford giving me a similarly penetrating and affectionate glance with his brown eyes.

But they did not at those moments exchange glances between the two of them. Whatever their feelings about me were, none of it had anything to do with their personal feelings about each other and certainly nothing to do with their association in the business of high finance. They seemed, in fact, to be two different people altogether when they met in their offices or in the boardroom. I think perhaps Father may have been somewhat disingenuous in this respect and only seemed to follow suit where Lewis was concerned. But certainly Lewis Shackleford, as was demonstrated by later events, put business first with all people. In the boardroom one would have thought he and Father were scarcely acquainted. There would be a decided deference shown Father when the question of the legality of any undertaking arose since he was officially legal counsel, but beyond that the eyes of the two men seldom met across the table. Though they were surely the two most powerful members present, they seemed to have the least to say. The other members might at times interrupt each other and even give way to shouting matches. But Father and Lewis would only smile at those other men's disagreements and would, themselves, never so much as raise their voices.

WHEN FATHER returned to Nashville after the death of my grandfather it had been with full understanding that he would devote all his talents and energies to Shackleford and Company. The firm had grown rapidly into an investment banking house and of course no longer dealt exclusively with municipal bonds. Shackleford and Company already owned controlling interest in several banks and insurance companies even then. I know that well before he left Thornton, Father had some tenuous connection or at any rate he had some dealings with the company and with Lewis Shackleford personally. I recall Mr. Shackleford's once having dinner with us in the old hip-roofed house that year when Grandfather lay dying in one of the upstairs rooms. And I remember what tremendous pleasure he took in the atmosphere of the place generally. He said with satisfaction that you could hardly stir about, there were so many Negroes on the place. After one meal, when the men sat talking endlessly, Father's old mammy, who ruled in the kitchen, came into the dining room and thumped Father on the head with her knuckles, saying: "You quit 'at talkin' and eat 'em victuals!" This filled Mr. Shackleford with such delight that he stood up from the table and put his arm around Mammy.

I don't know precisely on what business Mr. Shackleford had come to Thornton, but I know that it had to do with the sale or purchase of bonds issued by the West Tennessee and Forked Deer River Drainage District. And I know that that organization was created for the purpose of constructing drainage ditches all along the Forked Deer River and that those ditches would add hundreds of acres of good farmland in Thorn County. (I still have amongst my papers some of those old bonds, which of course are worthless and were defaulted upon only a few years after issuance.)

AFTER GRANDFATHER died, though I was only five at the time, I do remember the high good spirits with which Father set out for Nashville with what he must have considered the full complement of his family. I suppose it is because I sensed the importance of the day that I remember every detail of it so distinctly. We set out, as in our later moves, with two cars, the first driven by Father of course, the second by the black houseman and chauffeur Mac. We were followed, as usual, by two large vans. When Grandfather had ordered Father back to Thornton, the year before he died, he had insisted that Father lease his Nashville house and bring all his furniture—Mother's furniture, that is—with him. Since Father obeyed his father in almost all things, so far as I was able to observe, this was done. And since no additional furniture was needed in Grandfather's house, Mother's furniture was stored in the old farm office and in other of the brick dependencies that surrounded the house. Now, after Grandfather's death, it was all being returned to Nashville to be installed again in our house on Franklin Pike. That house, a relatively modest clapboard structure, though with extensive barns and stables, was set on the middle ground of a twenty-acre estate, an estate which adjoined the larger tract of land whereon Lewis Shackleford had his Georgian mansion. Since the key to our house was in the keeping of the Shacklefords, the plan was for us to go by their place to fetch it when we arrived.

We had left Thornton at eight in the morning and expected to arrive late in the afternoon. The distance was approximately one hundred fifty miles. But at nine that night we were still nine miles west of Nashville on what used to be known as Nine Mile Hill, and Father and Mac were out in the road patching an inner tube—repairing the ninth flat tire of the day. We children were exhausted and in depressed spirits. The vans had long since passed us, carrying Father's wardrobes and Mother's large pieces of Victorian furniture, and were no doubt already waiting in the driveway at our house. But Mother's spirits were still high enough to allow her to make jokes about the significance of the number nine. And Father was even playful about pumping up the tire, making noises with his mouth that led us to believe air was escaping again from the inner-tube patch. He had been like that all through the long day, never losing his temper, never getting out of patience with us children. There had been long stretches of dirt roads, and since it had rained the night before there was a great deal of mud. At least twice he and Mac had to get out and push the cars through the mire while Mother and Mac's wife, Mildred, got into the two driver's seats and steered. Inside the car we would sometimes hear Father—and see him through the rear window—shouting good-naturedly and even singing out "heave ho!" as he and Mac pushed us out of the worst of the muddy holes we got into. When we stopped for lunch at the little town of Dixon, Father told us joyfully that we would someday remember this journey as one of the great adventures of our life. We and our descendants, he said, would always remember it as the Carver family's historic migration to Nashville. Our descendants would someday go and put up markers where we had each of our flat tires! And all the while that he was giving us this food for thought, he was thinking to himself—at least one must so suppose—of the great adventure he was anticipating in the life that lay ahead of him in Nashville.

More than an hour after our last flat tire we had finally got through the sleeping city of Nashville. We were turning off the Franklin Pike onto the gravel lane that led to Lewis Shackleford's estate. As we drew up to the mansion there was not a light to be seen in any window. Father slipped out from behind the wheel of the front car, climbed the high front steps, and beat clamorously upon the door. "Knock, knock, knock! Sleep no more!" he called out playfully. "Macbeth does murder sleep!" He had come only to fetch the key to our house but he seemed determined to wake the entire household. And that was what he did. All at once lights appeared in half a dozen windows of the high brick façade. We heard a male voice inside shouting excitedly: "The Carvers are here!"

Presently a light came on in the ceiling of the big front gallery, and Mr. Lewis Shackleford was opening the heavy front door. Stepping out onto the gallery, he threw his arms about Father and commenced shouting to the rest of us: "Welcome, all of you Carvers!" And then Mrs. Shackleford appeared in the doorway and came out across the wide porch and down into the driveway to meet us. And presently she was followed by an old lady, who was her mother, and by three or four black servants, all of them carrying flashlights. They were like so many fireflies in the dark. Mother said afterward, with her ever-active sense of the past, that we were like travelers in the Tennessee wilderness a hundred years back being welcomed at the isolated cabin of a pioneer family. Even before the two men came out to where the cars were stopped in the lane Mrs. Shackleford was insisting that we all climb out and spend the night here. And Mr. Shackleford joined her, saying that the servants already had the beds "turned back." It was too late in the night, said Mrs. Shackleford, to be opening an empty house and setting up bedsteads for everybody. The moving men could shift for themselves and wait till we arrived in the morning to unload the vans. She would even send one of the servants over to tell them not to expect us tonight. Mildred and Mac were now delivered into the hands of those servants. Instructions were given for the care of the two dogs and the cat and the canary bird. I remember that as we got out of the car Mrs. Shackleford gave each of us children a hug, and Mr. Shackleford shook each of us formally by the hand. Since it happened that neither of our parents had brothers or sisters, it was as though at this significant moment in our lives we were acquiring our first uncle and aunt. For half a dozen years that relationship would seem an important reality. We would know their house, their stables, their wide acres almost as well as we knew our own. And now, fully awakened by the excitement of such a welcome as we were receiving, we made our way across the white gravel of the driveway and were ushered by the avuncular Lewis and the cordial Mary Ann Shackleford into the great hall of their house and then back into the dining room for a midnight supper. And after that we were led upstairs to the turned-back beds that awaited us.

IT WAS APPROXIMATELY six years later that Lewis Shackleford's deception and betrayal of my father came about. To us children it seemed a lifetime later. Perhaps it seemed so to my father, too—and to my mother. In my reinterpretation of Father's life and character—that is, after my sisters had moved back into the house with him and after Holly and I had once again settled down on 82nd Street—I tended to equate the significance of all his various worldly aspirations (and to equate all his subsequent successes). I recalled how against his own father's wishes Father had been determined to attend Vanderbilt University as an undergraduate. His father could think only of Princeton or Charlottesville for his son's education. But the young George Carver, in 1900, had recognized Vanderbilt as the rising university in the region where he was going to make his life. With his wonderful ego and soaring aspirations he wished to identify himself with that university. And of course he did so. He attended Vanderbilt and excelled there as a scholar and athlete. This must have represented his first profound satisfaction in his life, the first fulfillment of his aspiration to an otherness than that to which he had been born. Moreover, he afterward continued his studies through the law school there, again against his father's wishes. And although my grandfather had a puritanical distrust of politics and politicians, after law school and at the age of twenty-four the youthful George Carver returned again to Nashville as a member of the state legislature. This latter assured his being hired by one of the city's most prominent law firms. Meanwhile, he had dared to aspire to marriage with a girl who lived in one of those stone mansions that lined West End Avenue.

Until I came under the spell of Holly's new spirit of reconciliation—with family and with Father—such aspirations and achievements of my father had represented for me his willfulness, his selfishness, and even a certain ruthlessness. Now through Holly's influence I saw them as evidence of his imagination about himself and the kind of life he could make. He had now at last become a heroic figure in my eyes. It was his very oppositeness from me that I could admire without reservation, like a character in a book. At the age when I had been off to New York to lose myself in the collecting of musty old volumes and in the making of not very distinguished new books, my brave father had dared to stand in the lime-light of the state legislature, the youngest man ever elected to that body, he had aspired to the hand of a West End Avenue Nashville belle, he had presumed to set up as a corporation lawyer (*he*, the son of three generations of surveyors and old-fashioned land lawyers), and he had allowed himself to be drawn so far into the Nashville business establishment, or had so sought after that drawing in, that he found himself sitting virtually on the right hand of the youthful financial czar himself, Mr. Merriwether Lewis Shackleford.

It would be scarcely six years later that the young czar's empire would begin to totter. And it was approximately half-way through that period that Lewis Shackleford began in-volving Father in the affairs of insurance companies controlled by Shackleford and Company—in Cincinnati, in St. Louis, in Louisville. Soon Father found it necessary to spend three or four months at a time in those places, returning to Nashville only for long weekends with his family or for riding through the lanes with Lewis and other equestrian friends in their circle. Often there was not time for him to go downtown to "the company office" or time for an occasion when he could speak privately with Lewis about business matters. He would complain of this to Mother, who would remind him that what he came home for was to relax with his family and friends, not to talk business with Lewis.

Sometimes Mother would go with Father on his long sojourns to those more northern cities, and one spring they took Georgie and me along to St. Louis, where we were even put in school for a month or six weeks. I believe there was even some talk of the family's settling there permanently. Lewis thought that might be desirable. At any rate, toward the end of that fateful sojourn of ours in St. Louis the affairs of the insurance company there came to a crisis. It was discovered that certain large landholdings of the company in Missouri had been heavily mortgaged and that the money received, along with other funds of that company, had been transferred without Father's knowledge to other holdings of Shackleford and Company—other holdings, that is, that were in financial difficulties. Father and Mr. Shackleford were on the telephone daily and sometimes several times a day. Father had perfect confidence in Mr. Shackleford's being able to explain matters satisfactorily, and it ended by Lewis's agreeing to take a train to St. Louis in order to explain matters to the local board of directors. I went with Father to the Union Station to meet Lewis one morning, but he was not aboard the Nashville train. There were further telephone conversations during that day. Lewis had not been able to get away from the press of events in Nashville. He would come the next morning. Again I went with Father to the station, and again Lewis Shackleford was not on the train from Nashville.

We went a third morning to meet him, but when he did not arrive then there were no more communications between him and Father.

Within a few weeks we returned to Nashville and to our house on Franklin Pike. But still there was no communication between Father and Lewis. We would see one of the Shacklefords' limousines passing the entrance to our driveway, but none ever turned in. And we carefully lowered our eyes if some of us happened to be down near the entrance when one of the Shackleford limousines passed. Soon the newspapers were full of articles about the failure of Shackleford and Company, and there was already talk in our house about the family's removal to Memphis. Once my older sister Betsy suggested that Mr. Shackleford had sent Father off to St. Louis and Cincinnati just so he wouldn't be present to observe the dishonest goings-on. Father reprimanded her severely. He asked rhetorically whether Lewis might not have arranged matters as he did so that there could be no question of Father's involvement in such things as the transfer of funds. Soon there was an official investigation by the State of Tennessee. And it was true that neither the defense nor the prosecution asked Father to give testimony in the court actions that followed. After Betsy had made her offensive suggestion, Father told all four children that he wished never to hear of any of us mentioning Lewis Shackleford's name again. It would be a very long while indeed before we did so. It would be after we had for many years considered ourselves permanent residents of Memphis, and even then it would not be within Father's hearing.

IN MY REFLECTIONS on Father's past life, I made at least one observation that I had never before made. At first I made it only to myself. And not until several months later did

I convey the observation to Holly. With her reformed view
of how one should regard the conduct of one's parents she
found this new observation of mine altogether reprehensible
on my part. In fact, she went off to bed the night when I first
spoke my thoughts to her, stating explicitly that she wished
to sleep alone and asserting that she never again would will-
ingly discuss with me the subject of parents—aged, ailing, or
otherwise. The observation that so offended her was simply
this: All of Father's earlier aspirations and ambitions had required him to consider only the risk that might be entailed
for himself, but when he uprooted his family in Nashville and
took us to Memphis he was morally bound to consider the
risks there were for the psyches of five other people, not
merely a dependent young wife and a bundle of small children but a wife who was now past forty and four young
people who were either adolescents or young adults, the
youngest of them already in love with a dark-haired little
girl he had met at the annual horse show. I believe it is a
maxim beyond contradiction—and so I said to Holly at that
time—that high ambition and worldly aspirations are all very
well and even commendable so long as other persons are not
asked to share the risks created and confronted by the protag-
onist. This is true, so I felt at least and so I insisted to Holly,
for a father as well as for the chief of any tribe or nation. As
a man, it seemed admirable that Father had had the courage
and stamina to begin life over in early middle age. But *as* a
father, it came too late—as a father, that is, of three children
like Betsy and Josephine and myself. If we had all been un-
imaginative, insensitive children like Georgie, it would not of
course have mattered. In that case we would merely have felt
in our bones, as Georgie no doubt did, that our family life
had become a mess and would have managed somehow to
walk away from it—even if it meant getting ourselves killed.
The conclusion I drew from all this was not harsh. I felt that

Father's altogether human blindness could not be held against him. The dangerous ramifications that existed for his wife and children when he undertook to extricate himself from his embarrassing and humiliating situation in Nashville he could not have been expected to foresee. It was a hopeless situation for him, and one simply had to forget all that.

But Holly Kaplan would not have it so. It was not that she would have refused to applaud my forgiving him if forgiveness were called for, but forgetting was another matter altogether. In our midnight—and far past midnight—talks she continued to insist that merely forgetting would be to avoid the issue. From that she went on to insist that fathers were bound to be right in all disputations so far as their own children were concerned. At this point I could see that she was not really making sense. And I perceived of course that this nonsense of hers had something to do with the remorse or guilt she was feeling about her own father at the time. But I waited for Holly herself to say so, if it were to be said at all. Meanwhile, we went on and on in our debate. Could it really matter, though? I kept asking myself. Already I could see that my doctrine of forgetting was about as nonsensical as her reasoning that no forgetting was required. It was as if we were debating the question of how many angels could sit on the head of a pin. Or it was as if we were two Jews in the Temple debating some abstruse question of morality or perhaps two Christian Puritans, two Baptists or Methodists in the backwoods of Tennessee.

11

HOLLY AND I, one Saturday morning in late June, were lingering over our second or third cup of breakfast coffee. We heard the buzzing signal when the postman deposited our mail downstairs in the entryway. We looked at each other questioningly, each asking with his eyes if the other were going down to fetch the usually unrewarding Saturday mail. It was I who went down finally, riding the elevator of course, rather absentminded, hardly aware of what I was about. The box was crammed with bills and circulars and such. I fairly yanked it all out and slammed the box lid closed. I was already back on the elevator before I began glancing through the trash mail for the sight of a piece of first-class mail. And suddenly there it was, a letter from one of my sisters, the first since my wretched experience with them in March. I had to turn it over to see that it was from Josephine.

There had been postcards of the just-keeping-in-touch variety from both of them, but no letters. Somehow I had come to feel there would be no more letters—ever. But now I could almost see Josephine tripping down the asphalt driveway to the old-fashioned mailbox at the front gate, lifting the little metal flag to signal the "carrier" that she had placed a letter inside. How different, how much out of another world seemed her experience of posting the letter from mine of receiving it. As I fingered the envelope it seemed that it was a letter coming from the past. Even my last, hellish trip home seemed very remote in time. When presently I joined Holly in her little study, where she was still sipping cold coffee, I had the letter open and I read her the first sentences aloud:

Dear Phillip,

We have taken a cottage at Owl Mountain for the last two weeks in July. Father has seemed so frail and has been in such low spirits lately that we think he needs this change from the Memphis scene. Nothing would please him so much, of course, as would having you join us there. And I don't have to tell you how much Betsy and I would like it. . . .

At this point I handed the letter over to Holly, who, with her new concern for my relations with my father, read the rest of it aloud to me. It gave no details of just how frail Father was or how low were his spirits but gave many, many details of what the arrangements were for the stay at Owl Mountain, how many bedrooms and bathrooms the cottage had, whose cottage it was they had rented, and the plan for taking all meals at Owl Mountain Inn. When Holly put down the letter she said sympathetically: "I think you will have to go."

O w l M o u n t a i n is an old-fashioned watering spot in the Cumberland Mountains—or, as one sometimes says, on the

Cumberland Plateau. Whatever one calls it, this geographical feature is a fringe of low-lying mountains running more or less north and south and more or less dividing East Tennessee from Middle Tennessee. The little resort atop one of those hump-backed mountains is relatively near the Alabama and Georgia borders and is so near to Chattanooga—some forty miles—that scarcely anyone in that city would ever think of going there for a vacation. Nashville, on the other hand—some eighty miles northwest—is near enough for people to fancy keeping week-end cottages there, though seldom taking it seriously as a fashionable summer place. For Memphis, however, it is the nearest high ground within a distance of two hundred fifty miles and is therefore considered in some circles quite a fashionable place to go during July and August. When our family first moved to Memphis we used to laugh at the way people there spoke of going to Owl Mountain as though they were going to Asheville or Highlands or Hot Springs, Virginia. In those days my sisters would not have consented to go there under any circumstances. But now, as I supposed at least, it seemed a different matter to them. Many of their close friends spent the entire summer on the Mountain, and since the trip now was not much more than half a day's drive, they believed that even in his frail condition Father could quite easily make the trip.

Owl Mountain Inn, which as a matter of fact burned to the ground on a January night just six months after the events I am about to describe, had always been considered a potential firetrap. The fire is of no concern to us since it occurred afterward. I mention it only because one could not look at the old wooden structure without thinking: What a tinder-box! For many years no one had been willing to occupy the upstairs rooms. Only those on the ground floor were in use, and of course there was the dining room, which was immensely popular with the summer people. When my sisters took Father there those weeks in July and I came down to join them, the lobby and dining room of the hotel presented a lively scene.

I suppose the Owl Mountain community together with the Inn could accurately be called the last summer meeting place of the old-time denizens of Nashville and Memphis. The two cities long since seemed to have gone their separate ways and nowadays seemed scarcely aware of each other's existence. The influx of newcomers to those cities, swelling each nearly to a million inhabitants, no longer remembered that once upon a time both of the then small old cities had been peopled by members of the very same families. But in the dining room of Owl Mountain Inn one could still see old friends from the two places—and distant relatives—greeting each other cordially. Especially at midday dinner on Sunday one witnessed the spectacle. Sometimes even, at Sunday noon, there would be people, as I shall presently illustrate, who had driven all the way from Chattanooga or Knoxville just for old times' sake, only because some senior member of the family used to be brought to Owl Mountain as a small child.

I arrived in Owl Mountain on a Thursday, prepared to stay through the weekend. Due to peculiarities of flight schedules I flew to Knoxville and there rented a car, which I drove to the Mountain, a hundred miles distant. The days spent there with my father and sisters were quiet and for the most part uneventful. The spaciousness of the cottage was everything Josephine's letter had promised and that Betsy's letter a few days later had clearly confirmed. My first impressions upon arriving were that both sisters looked older than when I last saw them and even more like each other than in former times. But I realized very soon that this was because they both had stopped dyeing their hair. They also had gained considerable weight during the past four months. And yet since they were now dressing themselves more modestly and conservatively than they formerly had, the weight didn't seem to matter much.

Father, on the other hand, seemed to have shrunk. His hair was not so thick, and he seemed actually not to be as tall as he was just four months earlier. The features of his face seemed rougher and larger. If my sisters had got long in the tooth, so to speak, I remarked that he had got large in the ear. The four of us had little to occupy us except turning up for meals at the Inn and going for walks on the Grounds. Father even walked sometimes without his cane, and it was only then that one was aware of his uncertain step and his bad sight. Generally speaking, he did not seem really sick or unhappy but only waiting for something interesting to happen, and as always there was in his manner something that made one feel he was certain it *would* happen. At those times when we took our walks about the Grounds together and he was using his cane, I could see that he leaned pretty heavily upon it. We would rest frequently, sitting on one of the Grounds' benches or leaning against one of the ornamental stone arches that one came on now and again. We took all our meals at the Inn. At breakfast time or at lunch or dinner, a black waiter from the dining room would come out to the end of the front veranda and ring a large dinner bell that could be heard in the farthest reaches of the resort Grounds. Wherever we were, Father and I, we would then set out for the Inn, and of course we would always find Betsy and Josephine waiting for us at our assigned table and usually waving to us the length of the long, high-ceilinged dining room as we entered.

ON SUNDAY, before I was to drive back to Knoxville in the afternoon, we went of course to the Inn for midday dinner. My sisters insisted upon wearing hats for that meal, though Father and I laughed at them about it. They did so because all other women would be wearing hats, too. The churchgoers usually came directly from church in their proper church hats, and it was the custom for Owl Mountain women who didn't attend church (there were others like us who were not churchgoers) to wear hats to Sunday dinner, out of respect for those who did attend services. Even as Father and I crossed the room, with the leather heels of Father's white-and-brown wing-tipped shoes clacking on the highly polished pine floor, I had the feeling that I had caught a glimpse of a familiar face at a table in the front corner of the room. After we were seated I stole a glance in that direction. I am not sure which face I had caught sight of as we crossed the dining room, whether it was that of Clara Price or that of Clara Price's teenaged daughter. I don't know which of the two looked the more or the less like the Clara Price I had known.

The first thing I did was to count the number of other children at their table. There were five altogether, and none of them less than a teenager. Then I looked at Clara's face. It was lined and thin but still quite beautiful, I thought. And then there was the father of the children. (I couldn't manage the word "husband.") He was white-haired and sleek, I said to myself, and in his dark pin-striped summer suit he was the epitome of what Clara and I used to call "Chattanooga proper." Here they all were in their togetherness, a Chattanooga family who had no doubt driven over from the West Brow of Lookout Mountain for a Sunday dinner at "the picturesque Owl Mountain Inn." From the first moment of course the question was whether or not I should go over and speak to her. It was a question really of whether it would be more awkward to confess to my father and sisters who it was over there and to go over and be introduced all round or more awkward to say nothing and to keep my eyes carefully averted throughout the dinner hour. Somehow I got through the ordering of the meal and being served. And then I ate heartily, as if to forget all else. The difficulty now would be the escape from the room without ever coming to a decision on what was least awkward. That was what I yearned to do. But there was only fifteen minutes of that agony, because from the moment that I took my last bite of floating island, matters were out of my hands.

"Can I believe my eyes, Phillip," I heard Betsy saying, "or is that not your old friend Clara Price over there?" Then I heard Josephine say: "Why, you know, I'm absolutely sure it is!" Without pretending to turn and look, without lifting my eyes from my plate, I said: "That's who it is, my dear sisters." Then while my eyes were still lowered, a terrible thought struck me, an inescapable truth about the meddling interference of my old-maid sisters came home to me and a new insight as to the lengths they had been willing to go to revenge themselves upon their father, to wound him most deeply, to divide him forever from his two sons.

Presently I looked up at Betsy, and then at Josephine, who was seated on the other side of Father. Underneath their black straw Sunday hats the faces of both the two dowdy women were crimson. I didn't have to ask: "How did you know it was Clara Price? When did you ever have opportunity to see her?" It had swept over me before I looked up that not only my father had made a trip to Chattanooga to see my beloved Clara those many years ago during the War. My sisters Betsy and Josephine had gone possibly before Father, or possibly afterward, to try to persuade her to marry me in defiance of Father's stern wishes, and the impression they had made on her with all the finery of their attire and all the fury of their defiance of Father had been decisive in Clara's choosing to take flight as she did from the scene. Or had it been something else they did, something more than the mere impression of

what they were like? A few years later they would give me
money to disobey Father and go off to New York. Had there
possibly been an offer of money to Clara, to make our getting
married possible? All this was not merely a sudden suspicion
on my part. I felt it was sudden knowledge. It did not even
occur to me of course to wonder whether Father might also
have recognized Clara Price. I knew that his bad eyesight
would have precluded that. Yet I think as we sat there I might
have given way to a self-revealing rage at both my father and
my sisters had not, just then, something even more momentous occurred to distract us all.

Suddenly my sister Josephine bent her large-bosomed
torso forward over the dinner dishes that were still on the
table. Since my eyes were already fixed on her I was able to
observe the change as her heavy visage went from the crimson caused by Betsy's revelation to a pale and positively ashen
hue. She was staring directly into Betsy's eyes, and it was
Betsy alone whom she addressed. "Clara Price is nothing!"
she fairly wailed. "You can't see who it is at that table over
against the wall with all those Nashville young people and
who has now risen to his feet and is coming toward us!" I do
not know whether Father, with his failing sight, would have
recognized this person even as he drew closer to us if Josephine had not after a little pause for breath spoken his name.
"It's Mr. Lewis Shackleford!" she said with precisely the
horror of someone suddenly identifying a ghost.

The old man was leaning on a cane when he came
shambling up to us, and he was wearing a pince-nez on his
long nose—a pince-nez with a black ribbon attached which
fell down about his shoulders and around the stiff collar of his
white shirt. His brown eyes—with little specks flashing in
them—were so magnified by the thick lenses of his spectacles
that at first I noticed almost nothing else about him. In the
next seconds I saw that he was totally bald now and that his

ears and nose, like my father's, seemed to have greatly en-
larged. But he was dressed with the same care he had always
exercised—in the Nashville manner of course—the same
starched white shirt, the gold cuff links, the natural linen suit,
the white shoes, the navy-and-white polka-dot tie. I saw
beyond any doubt that he *was* Lewis Shackleford. Then I
saw what I could hardly believe. My father rose from the
table, took two steps forward to meet him, and the two tall
and still very straight old men threw their arms about each
other in such an ardent embrace that I felt myself on the
verge of bursting into tears. I might actually have done so
had I not at that instant looked over at Betsy and Josephine.
They sat dry-eyed, gazing at each other for a moment and
then glaring almost threateningly at me. It took only that to
make me remember the ugly significance the moment held
for all three of us. Again, and despite my intention really, I
cast a furtive glance in the direction of Clara Price and her
family. Either they were or they pretended to be unaware of
the reunion taking place at our table. But all the rest of the
Sunday diners in the big room—the Nashville and the Memphis people—had their eyes trained on us and were aware of
nothing else at that moment. Presently Father pulled away
from Mr. Shackleford and turned to exclaim to our middle-
aged threesome: "Will you look who's here, children!" We
acknowledged his exclamation only with solemn nods of our
heads and at last with the lowering of our eyes to the de-
spoiled remnants of food on our dinner plates.

I AM NOT CERTAIN how Mr. Shackleford responded
to our lowered eyes that Sunday noon. He had undoubtedly
had many people turn their eyes away from him since the
days of his glory. The others at his table were—or so it was

speculated by my sisters—his own nephews and nieces and great-nephews and -nieces. Apparently he was as fond as ever of young people. We all knew that his wife Mary Ann had been dead for a number of years, and that he lived now in a modest but very charming old house in the village of Franklin. We had heard it said that he entertained at lunch every Saturday the most interesting and promising young men in the business and professional world of Nashville. I do not know, either, how Father responded to our lowered eyes. But my father no doubt counted still, as always in the past, on events finally turning out favorably for him. He very likely told himself that we would come round in the end and accept this reconciliation between him and his old friend.

Father took his crook-cane from the back of the high-backed oak chair in which he had been sitting, and the two old men with their canes and their leather-heeled shoes went noisily off across the pine floor, talking as if their old flow of conversation had never been interrupted and exchanging between themselves repeated glances of admiration and affection, Father through his horn-rims, Lewis through the black-rimmed pince-nez. I felt that everyone in the room except Clara and her family, who still had eyes only for one another, was staring at the two old men and at us. Betsy said: "I know this has been painful for you, Phillip. Jo and I got you into it, and we'll get you out." She was referring of course to Clara's presence. And presently she and Josephine came up on either side of me, took me by the arm, and as we walked toward the lobby doorway they pretended to be making animated conversation with me. They imagined that I was suffering from the proximity of Clara Price and her family. Yet all the while I was discovering that I actually did not care a fig for their presence, that I could have, without any feeling at all, gone over and presented myself or I could, as it was, just as easily have not done so. I was discovering that all I cared about now was how I had been treated by my family in the long-ago affair of Clara Price. It was a painful discovery and realization, for it caused a deep hurt to know that about myself. Looking ahead at the two old men and half listening to the chatter of my sisters on either side of me, I could think only that indirectly at least it was this Lewis Shackleford who had affected my life so that I would become a man who would find it so difficult to fall in love with a woman that it could happen only once in my life. I felt my narrowness and cowardice about love was all due, inadvertently or otherwise, to my father's treatment of me and Lewis's treatment of my father. I hated the skinny old man walking there beside Father. I felt the impulse to shake my two stout, behatted sisters off my arms and dash forward and push the two old fellows apart. What right had they to such satisfaction as this reunion apparently gave them?

Instead, I said nothing to Betsy and Josephine about this impulse of mine. When we got into the lobby we saw that Father and Lewis had passed out onto the front veranda and were now seating themselves in two rockers out there. Betsy pointed silently to a side door. We slipped out through that door, across the side veranda, and down the flight of wooden steps to the gravel path that led to our cottage. Nearly an hour later Father joined us on the cottage porch, having been led to our front steps by one of Lewis Shackleford's great-nephews. We all four sat on the porch and talked for another hour before I got into my rented car to drive to the Knoxville airport. But while we sat there none of us made any mention of the people we had seen in the dining room. It was as though the whole episode had been an unhappy dream, and it was indeed so much like the bad dreams one has that when I was alone in the rented car and later in my seat on the plane I could almost doubt its reality.

WHEN SIX WEEKS later a new set of telephone calls came to me from Memphis there was no question as to whether or not I would go down there. Holly said of course that I must go. "He needs you now if ever he did," she said. And there wasn't a doubt in my own mind. It seems that every week since their reunion at Owl Mountain, Father and Lewis had held long, rambling exchanges over the telephone between Nashville and Memphis. And sometimes one of them would call back the following day to say something he had forgotten to mention earlier or to produce a name neither of them had been able to think of. It had been the source of mounting irritation to both sisters, hearing Father's old voice droning on and on, and his "yes . . . yes . . . yes," and periodically his blast of laughter that seemed to have more vigor in it than anything else about him nowadays.

But now Lewis had invited Father to come for a visit to Nashville—to Franklin, that is—for an extended visit of six weeks or more. Who knows, said Betsy, it might be extended indefinitely if both of the old fellows should manage to live beyond the six weeks. Speaking more seriously, she added, who would look after him if Father had a bad seizure of neuropathy while in Franklin and who would give him his daily blood tests or his insulin injections? Even in an emergency neither she nor Josephine was going to come to Nashville and stay in the house of Lewis Shackleford! The answer was that the current houseman and chauffeur, Horace, would drive him to Franklin and remain there as long as Father chose to stay. And Betsy's old-fashioned response, worthy of her Nashville grandmother, was: "Pshaw! What good would that no-good Horace be in a real emergency?" The wish was for me to come and put my foot down on such a plan or to persuade the doctor to do so. The doctor was not now being at all cooperative. He didn't seem to realize how difficult even the ride to Nashville would be for Father. Why, on the trip to Owl Mountain the old man had been on the verge of an insulin reaction, and they had had to spend the last hours of the journey feeding him fruit and candy bars.

I had not told Holly Kaplan of the impulse I had had in the dining room of the Inn—that is, the impulse to use violence in separating the two old men. When I had returned from Owl Mountain, I found her in such a depressed state about her own father's health that I saw no reason to go into my own strange emotions. By this time it was known that her father was dying of cancer. There had been two operations, and it had been decided that there would be no more. Two weeks after I returned, she flew out to Cleveland. But she found her father so surrounded by her brothers and sisters that she could scarcely get to his bedside. She came back to New York almost immediately, in an even worse frame of mind than before. I could not tell her about my new feelings of resentment against my own father and against Mr. Lewis Shackleford.

When Holly said that I must go to Father she meant that I must go in order to help him disregard my sisters' wishes and to assist in his escape to Franklin. And so I flew to Memphis again and made the flight on still another Monday morning. I don't think I knew, myself, what my own intentions were. By this time of course I accepted Holly's doctrine that our old people must be not merely forgiven all their injustices and unconscious cruelties in their roles as parents but that any selfishness on their parts had actually been required of them if they were to remain whole human beings and not become merely guardian robots of the young. This was something to be remembered, not forgotten. This was something to be accepted and even welcomed, not forgotten or forgiven.

I could not imagine myself trying to prevent Father's and

Horace's setting out toward Nashville and Franklin that afternoon, as they were planning to do, but neither could I imagine myself assisting in Father's reconciliation with that man
whose name we had all through the years been forbidden to
mention and whose mistreatment of Father had been the cause
of all our frustration and maladjustment. When I came inside
the terminal in Memphis, Alex of course was again waiting
for me. As we drove under and over all the various expressways on the route to Father's house our efforts at conversation
were frequently interrupted by the carelessness of other driv-
ers, but I felt that Alex was unduly distracted by the traffic.
"He needs you now if ever he did." It was of course exactly
the same thing that Holly had said to me—the very words.
When I made no reply to Alex, he waited a few moments
and then changed the subject. I remember he talked about his
own children more affectionately than he had used to do. He
said that his boy Howard had been in difficulty with the law
lately, said that the boy really seemed to have bad luck in
everything. We arrived at the entrance to Father's driveway
at precisely two o'clock. That was the hour that he and
Horace were scheduled to set out for Nashville.

As Alex pulled his old Chevrolet under Father's porte
cochere I saw Horace slowly bringing Father's Buick convertible up from the garage. I was not unaware—and I don't
believe Alex could have been—that only through the porte
cochere could the big Buick automobile pass on into the front
driveway and so out through the entrance gateway to Poplar
Pike. Nevertheless, I promptly hopped out of the car and
started for the side door. But suddenly I halted and looked
back at Horace and the Buick again. And without thinking
what I was saying almost, I called out to Alex to come with
me and to bring his car keys. What I said caused me to stop
there for a split second longer. Because it was only when I
had spoken to Alex about his keys that I became aware of

my own intentions. And then I was filled with doubt again
about what my intentions were. I cannot remember ever
being less sure of my own aims. Presently Alex and I, he with
his keys, rushed on through the side door of the house. Inside,
there was silence. Or at any rate in the front rooms and
during the first moments there was silence.

The silence that greeted us was disturbing to me. As the
two of us stood together in the living room I felt that I was
more the stranger in this house than Alex. Somehow it was
the silence that kept me from pushing on into the back part
of the house where the bedrooms were. I assumed that Father
must be about to leave, and so finally I stepped into the center
hallway and called out to him. Immediately Josephine came
hurrying up from the bedroom wing. She took me by the
arm and without in any way acknowledging Alex's presence
led me back into the living room, through the outside door of
which I had just entered the house. "Betsy is lying down,"
she said. "She's not well. Her blood pressure has shot way
up—that is, with all this excitement Father is creating."

"I didn't know Betsy had high blood pressure," I said.

"It's nothing special," she said, smiling significantly up at
me. "At our age we all have something, don't we?"

"Certainly we are all of us too old for such goings-on as
this," I said. I looked at her skeptically, because I knew it
was something she had made up on the spur of the moment.

While we were speaking, Father appeared in the wide
doorway to the dining room. He held his hat in one hand and
his cane in the other. His tan polo coat was thrown over his
arm. He wore a broad smile of a kind one wasn't accustomed
to seeing on his face. It seemed to say: *I'm* not too old for
such goings-on. He seemed thoroughly ready for the trip to
Nashville, ready for any eventuality. He was counting still on
his luck. Presently he said: "What on earth are you doing

here, Phillip?" Then he looked at Josephine and said simply:
"Oh." And then after a few seconds he looked at me and pro-
nounced the very same "Oh." He came on into the living
room then and looked out a side window to where Alex's old
Chevrolet was stopped in the porte cochere. He smiled at me,
and I couldn't tell for sure whether or not there was irony in
it. "I am afraid your car is in my car's way," he said to me,
knowing perfectly well of course that it was Alex's car.

I looked out the window too and after a moment I said:
"Yes, I'm afraid it is." Father eased himself into a chair, and
I said: "We'll be moving it shortly," not knowing, myself,
whether I meant it or not.

"Oh, good," Father said, giving me that smile again—
rather more vaguely this time.

We exchanged a few sentences about the weather then,
the four of us did. It was beautiful, bright fall weather, we
said, perfect for travel. It was almost beyond belief, I added.
Father threw back his head and laughed at that reflection.
Then he looked at me very seriously and said: "It really is,
you know."

"How this town has grown," I said, to change the subject.
"I haven't seen so many expressways anywhere. Even Alex had
trouble finding his way here from the airport," I said, though
of course this was untrue. We sat exchanging such common-
places and untruths for twenty minutes or so. Once I looked
out the window and saw Horace out there with his chauffeur's
cap held under his armpit while he examined Alex's car—to
see if the keys were in it, I think. They weren't there, of
course. And now Alex had absentmindedly placed the ring
of keys Horace was looking for around his left thumb. He
was jangling them ever so slightly. And so I observed the
keys were safely in his keeping.

For a moment I debated saying that I would take the keys

out to Horace so that he could move the car if he wished. I don't know whether I meant it or not. But I hadn't yet decided about this when we heard the telephone ringing in the back part of the house. Presently someone answered it, and I supposed correctly that it was Betsy. Then I heard her walking very fast up the hallway toward us. She came into the living room and went directly to Father. Without looking at me or Josephine, she perched herself on the arm of his chair. "Father," she said, placing one hand on his shoulder as if she were talking to a child, "there has been a call from Nashville." After that she sat there for what seemed an interminable time, saying nothing more, only gazing down into Father's face. Finally she said: "There is bad news about poor Mr. Shackleford." She waited a moment for this to register on him. Then she looked slowly around at our faces to see if it was registering on us. Meanwhile, Father removed his horn-rimmed glasses in the way he had of doing when he was most serious about something. "He died in his sleep last night," Betsy said. "It is assumed it was a heart attack. Anyway, it's a blessing it came when he was asleep."

"I don't believe it!" Father declared belligerently. He replaced his glasses and then turned his eyes first to Josephine and then to me to see if we believed it or if we were in on such a hoax.

"You know I wouldn't lie about something like that," Betsy said. She stood up but kept her hand on his shoulder.

"No, I suppose you would not," he said under his breath.

"Maybe you should come back and lie down for a while," Betsy said to him. Glaring out the window at Horace, she added: "I'll go out and tell Horace to come in and help." She went out through the side door, and I could see her out there talking to Horace, who presently came into the house by way of the back door. Meanwhile, Josephine and I went over to

Father. Jo got down on her knees and placed her hand on his, which rested still on the chair arm. "I'm sorry, dear," she said. "I know it seems ironic it should come at this time." He gave a deep sigh but showed no other sign of emotion. Her hand remained on his. Presently he placed his other hand on top of hers. And then she placed *her* other hand on top of that hand. They looked at each other, dry-eyed and without much expression in their faces. With their hands like that it was as though they were measuring to see who would have the first turn at bat. I almost expected Father to pull out his bottom hand and place it on top, though of course he did not. The fact is, we were all dry-eyed, or all, I think, except Alex. It was then he who got up and went over to the window, and without looking back at me he said: "I want to see you again, Phillip. There's something I'd like to talk with you about." He opened the glass door that led to the porte cochere and went out without saying goodbye to any of us. Presently Father said in the steadiest voice imaginable: "What's come over Alex? He didn't say hello *or* goodbye to me."

A F T E R H O R A C E H A D got Father to his bed, my first speculation was on whether I could get a plane back to New York that night. But I thought better of it, of course. They made up the bed in Father's study for me, and I telephoned Alex to tell him what time I'd be ready in the morning. Betsy and Josephine and I had a little supper together in the break-fast room, and Father had something brought to him in his own bedroom. But next morning we all had breakfast to-gether, and though neither Betsy nor Jo had much to say, the two of *them* seemed to me as fit as a fiddle. I thought to myself: Why, for them this was just another inning! Even Father seemed to have recovered his good spirits and was not dwelling at all on Mr. Shackleford's death. The morning paper was late in coming, and Father asked Josephine to get the paper's circulation desk on the telephone and give those people a piece of her mind. She did so with great alacrity— even with great gusto, I might say. I thought at first she was raising her voice unnecessarily with the poor circulation clerk and then I realized that it was done mostly for the benefit of Father, who was off in the other room and would have had difficulty hearing her and taking his satisfaction if she had not raised her voice.

When we went into the living room after breakfast I found myself admiring the way the old man carried himself. He wasn't using his cane. He stood very straight by the living-room fireplace and rested his elbow on the mantel shelf. How often I had seen him stand like that! I plopped down in a comfortable chair opposite him. There was no self-pity in his face and no regret. He seemed merely a man thinking of what he was going to do with himself this day and perhaps tomorrow. His friend Lewis Shackleford was dead. His plans were all canceled. But he would have to occupy himself until there was some other occasion for action on his part. Suddenly it didn't seem to be my father at all, standing there before me, but a man of no particular relation to me and of no particular age. He was a man with the strength still to accept whatever fate brought him and to take advantage of whatever opportunities large or small that there might be for his talents. Presently he said to me: "How long are you going to stay with us this time, Phillip?"

"Oh, I have to go back today, Father," I said. "Alex is coming to take me to the airport."

"Of course he is!" he said. And he threw back his head and gave a quick little laugh that was quite literally nothing more than a mere "ha-ha." Then he went on, having dismissed that subject. "Alex is a strange fellow," he said, and I was reminded of what he had said yesterday about Alex's saying neither hello nor goodbye to him.

"Alex has his moods, like the rest of us," I said by way of explanation though not necessarily the correct explanation. Alex had simply been too unhappy with events to indulge in greetings or leave-takings.

After a moment Father said: "I suppose it is he who always summons you home when I seem about to bolt."

"Well . . . yes." I felt I had no reason to drive a deeper wedge between Father and my sisters, if in fact a wedge was there. And so I said nothing about their letters and their calls. "It may not seem so to you," I said, "but I come always in the hope of assisting you."

"And that is Alex's wish—for you and for himself?"

"Oh, he's your chief ally," I said. "Next to me, of course." He gave me a smile that was both speculative and reflective of genuine amusement. I felt that our communication at this moment was the nearest we had ever come to communication directly on any serious matter. And I felt an admiration for him I had not felt since I was a small boy. And yet as we sat there I thought silently: Well, we have got our revenge on you, I suppose—Betsy and Josephine and I. Right and wrong doesn't enter into it. The urge has been beyond reason and beyond our control. Presently he took a step forward and toward me, and I got up from my chair. He took my hand and said:

"Goodbye, Phillip. Come back home soon."

It was just as though this had been an ordinary visit. And then he turned and went off to his room.

By the time I brought my bag up from Father's study, where I had slept, to the front part of the house, Alex was waiting in the porte cochere. I don't know how long he had been there. He didn't give any signal of his presence. I suppose he didn't feel up to seeing my family that morning. He had just driven in quietly and waited for me to discover him. As I came out and got into the car I noticed what I hadn't noticed yesterday, that his Chevrolet was indeed a very old model with several large dents that had obviously been painted over by an amateur. I reflected that anyone but Alex would have apologized for its appearance. But he didn't seem to mind or even to be aware that he drove a battered-up old car.

I WAITED HALF the distance to the airport before asking what Alex had on his mind that he wished to talk to me about. "I wasn't sure you would want to hear it, after all," he said, as if he had real misgivings about going into the matter. "You had a hard day yesterday," he said. "All of you did. I'll write you a letter about the other thing."

"No, let's hear about it now," I said. "Maybe I'll find it a needed distraction."

"You won't—not exactly," he said. Then he began telling me his harebrained scheme. He approached the subject cautiously, making several references to his own anticipated retirement from the University, which, as it turned out, was fifteen or twenty years away of course. His scheme was that I should retire from my publishing house job and give what he termed my "fabulous collection of rare books" to Memphis State University. He had looked into the matter and found that they would almost certainly build a special room in the library to house "the Phillip Carver Collection." I would be made curator of the collection and on the strength of my gift I would most likely be given a senior appointment of some kind to teach courses in the collecting of rare books and/or general courses in the making of new books—"the physical production." During most of this silly discourse of his I sat in the front seat beside him, simply shaking my head in disapproval. But it was actually still going on when we got inside the airport terminal. And even as I left him to get aboard my plane, he was still talking that same nonsense.

12

WHEN I ARRIVED at 82nd Street late that afternoon I found Holly in her study, reading proof. As I stepped into the doorway of the room, she looked up, startled, as if she had not heard me enter the apartment, almost as if she didn't know who I was, standing there. She removed her reading glasses and peered across the room. She was waiting of course for me to speak first. But I couldn't say anything. I felt empty of thoughts and words. At last with furrowed brow and a look of intense concern in her eyes, she asked: "Did you arrive in time to help? Did Father make his escape?" It seemed absurd of her to be referring to that man she had never seen as "Father." I felt that from now on she would refer to all men twice her age as "Father." She might even begin referring to me as "Father," as though that would make up for her having left her own father and come to live with me.

"Yes, I arrived in time," I said at last, "but just as the old man was about to set out, word came that Lewis Shackleford was dead of a heart attack."

She dropped the galley proof she was holding in her lap. And she allowed her head to fall backward and come to rest on the chair back. "Oh, God . . . Oh, God," she said in an almost soundless whisper. "What a terrible trick for fate to play!" I did not tell her that had I not arrived when I did, Father would certainly have got away, that he might at least have been able to attend Lewis's funeral, that my arrival actually delayed him till it was too late for him to go, because there could be no setting out once we all knew Lewis was dead. And now Holly was saying: "I am so very sorry, Phillip. I know what suffering it must have caused you. But you did what you could. It's the most any of us can do." Now *she* was talking nonsense too. I turned away and said I was going to fix us each a drink. I came back presently with our usual, sensible, weak little scotch and water, one apiece for us.

Before I sat down I suddenly said to myself: This is how it is to be from now on. And I found it did not displease me to think so. With equal sadness and almost without thought of what I was doing, I brought out my wallet and took from it the gold clover-leaf pendant. "Here is something you might enjoy wearing," I said. "It belonged to my mother, and it's supposed to bring you good luck." My implication was that it was something I had just brought from home. Holly held it in the palm of her hand for a moment and then she, the person who cared nothing for jewelry or trinkets, said what was the least she could say, I suppose: "It's really rather pretty, isn't it?"

"Yes, I think so," I said.

She held it up by its little chain and looking at it through squinted eyes she said: "I have the feeling I've seen it before amongst your things. You must have had it a very long time."

It had never occurred to me until now that Holly ever looked "amongst my things." She had of course seen it in my bureau drawer, where I often kept it. I didn't keep it in my wallet in any systematic way but only most of the time and through long habit. She had seen it in my drawer, and I could tell from the way she spoke that she had surmised it had to do with someone else. But I could also tell from the expression on her face that she didn't mind. And it occurred to me then for the first time that there had probably been a male equivalent of Clara Price in Holly's earlier life. Of course there had. And I was happy to realize that *I* didn't mind about that. In our tenth-floor, 82nd Street serenity we were well beyond such petty jealousies. Presently Holly slipped the pendant into the pocket of her dress and took up her drink. And we sat there in the twilight and sipped our drinks while we talked our own combined nonsense together, each his or her own brand of inconclusive nonsense about the reconciliation of fathers and children, talked on and on until total darkness fell and it was time once again to put on lights there in our Manhattan apartment and take up the galleys of print we had yet to read.

OUR CONCLUSIONS and resolutions were all nonsense, of course. But one sensible thing I did manage. Two days after I returned to New York I telephoned Father. At first we were uncomfortable in our rather vapid exchanges. I have never been very good on the telephone. But finally we got into talk about those distant times when I trailed after him and Lewis Shackleford when they were fox hunting in the Radnor Hills or swimming at Franklin. It gave me special satisfaction to use Lewis Shackleford's name casually in conversation with Father. After that, we talked about people in Nashville I only vaguely remembered. I had only to mention a name, and that would set him off. It was somehow a pleasure to imagine my two sisters listening to his reminiscences uneasily in the next room to where he was talking. Very soon I comprehended that I was taking Lewis Shackleford's place on the telephone. And I felt the satisfaction there was in it for both of us.

I called him again a week later, and my second call was no less successful. We talked about Mother and her sense of humor and sense of history. From that time on I called him every week. Or sometimes he called me. On the long-distance telephone we were able to speak of things we had never been able to talk about face to face. I can't say why this was so, not for certain. Often it would seem to me that it was not my father I was talking with but some other man who was very much like him. Or I would find myself visualizing him not as he looked now but as he looked when I was in my teens or even younger. The calls were indeed such a tremendous satisfaction for me that sometimes I would stay home from the ballet or the theater or from an exhibition at the Morgan Library, for instance, because I had the premonition that Father might telephone while I was out that evening. And often as not I was correct in my premonition.

MY FATHER DIED of a stroke the following spring. Holly's died also during that winter. Of course each of us had to go to the funeral—Holly to Cleveland, I to Memphis. Holly tried to make herself stay over in Cleveland a few days in order to fight with her brothers and sisters, out of duty, about various possessions, but in the end she could not make herself do it. She couldn't even pretend to care the way she would have *had* to pretend if she had stayed over. Instead, she returned to the serenity of 82nd Street. As for me, I had no such impulse. After the two dead men's wills were probated, many months later, Holly and I were then quite well off and with our means we might have moved into a larger, brighter apartment and discarded all our ugly used furniture if we had chosen to. But we agreed that it hardly seemed worth all the trouble, hardly worth all the upheaval of our papers and books.

And so Holly and I are still here. And my sisters are still occupying my father's house, like two spinsters in the last century, with the family servants still there to look after them. Though they have written me several times that they think of moving back into one of their own houses at midtown and even of returning to their real estate business, I am confident that they never will. The old charade would no longer have its significance, and they seem to have nothing else to live for. Since I no longer hear from Alex Mercer, I can only suppose that he and his wife, Frances, are settled—a little smug and a little disappointed—at their hearthside, a sort of Memphis Darby and Joan, cared for by their children. (I am still not sure just how many there are.) Perhaps even their son Howard has mended his ways somewhat and devotes himself to caring for the old folks.

As for Holly and me, I don't know what the end is to be of two people like us. We have our serenity of course and we have put Memphis and Cleveland out of our lives. Those places mean nothing to us nowadays. And surely there is nothing in the world that can interfere with the peace and quiet of life in our tenth-floor apartment. I have the fantasy that when we get too old to continue in the magazine and book trade the two of us, white-haired and with trembly hands, will go on puttering amongst our papers and books until when the dusk of some winter day fades into darkness we'll fail to put on the lights in these rooms of ours, and when the sun shines in next morning there will be simply no trace of us. We shall not be dead, I fantasize. For who can imagine he will ever die? But we won't for a long time have been "alive enough to have the strength to die." Our serenity will merely have been translated into a serenity in another realm of being. How else, I ask myself, can one think of the end of two such serenely free spirits as Holly Kaplan and I?

A NOTE ON THE TYPE

This book was set on the Linotype in Janson, a recutting made direct from type cast from matrices long thought to have been made by the Dutchman Anton Janson, who was a practicing type founder in Leipzig during the years 1668–87. However, it has been conclusively demonstrated that these types are actually the work of Nicholas Kis (1650–1702), a Hungarian, who most probably learned his trade from the master Dutch type founder Dirk Voskens. The type is an excellent example of the influential and sturdy Dutch types that prevailed in England up to the time William Caslon developed his own incomparable designs from them.

Composed by Maryland Linotype Composition Company, Baltimore, Maryland. Printed and bound by R. R. Donnelley & Sons, Harrisonburg, Virginia.

Typography and binding design
by Dorothy Schmiderer